ARSHANA

a novel

by

Indrani Gayadeen

To dear Dr. Khan
from Indra

IOWI

ISBN: 978-1-926926-88-9

Cover image:
Copyright: https://www.123rf.com/profile_subbotina

Published by:
In Our Words Inc. /inourwords.ca / inourwords2008@gmail.com
251 Queen Street South, Suite #561, Streetsville, ON L5M 1G7

DEDICATION

This book is dedicated to my husband,
Dr. Donald Gayadeen,
who not only inspired me,
but encouraged me to live by the old saying,
"To whom much is given, much is expected."
I have been blessed
with much more than I ever expected,
and now it is my turn to give back.

1

I often look back to the day I met Arshana and wonder if Fate had destined it to play out the way it did, down to the little details of time and setting. It was one of those beautiful days in the middle of June, neither too hot nor windy. The huge maple overhead offered me ample protection from the sun. I adjusted the lounge to a more comfortable position, laid back and closed my eyes.

During the summer months, I tried to spend as much time as possible in my garden. My favorite time of day was just before noon when I could lay back and enjoy the soft purple shadow of the sun as it shone directly above my head. How lucky I was, I thought to myself, to be able to enjoy the beautiful surroundings, the fresh air, the peace and solitude.

Usually I would drift into sleep, but today my thoughts kept wandering. I began to reflect on my life.

My friends would often say to me, "Ruth you are always so calm: you never ever seem to have a problem."

My reply was always the same, "If I have a problem, I put it in God's hands."

I had a few rough patches in my life but nothing really to complain about. All in all, it had been a good life with all the comforts money could buy.

My only regret was that my husband Solomon was no longer there to share it with me. He died a year after our son David graduated from medical school.

David was a bright student. Always at the top of his class. He was his father's pride and joy, and when Dr. Don Taylor, one of Mississauga's most respected physicians offered him a position in his family practice, Solomon was elated. He would boast about his son to anyone who would listen. And then one evening, at a barbecue at a friend's home, our whole world fell apart. Without any warning, Solomon suffered a massive heart attack. Paramedics were called and they did their best to save him, but Solomon never recovered. He died in the ambulance on the way to the hospital.

David was devastated by his father's death. He suffered in silence but thank God, we had lots of good friends who stood by us at the time of our grief, and gradually David and I were able to re-adjust.

The warm weather was beginning to take its toll on me. I began to feel groggy, so I decided that whether I fell asleep or not, I was going to close my eyes and enjoy the rest of the day. But apparently, it wasn't meant to be. First a squirrel jumped on my chair, startling me and himself, before he scampered off. Then a couple of blue jays flew onto a branch above my head. Flossy's continuous barking and rattling of the gate didn't help one bit. Flossy always behaved in that manner when there was someone or something at the gate. I got up, folded my chair and placed it against the trunk of the tree; making sure that I did not touch René's orchids. They were in full bloom and they grew close to the roots of the tree.

I was walking slowly towards the gate to see what all the commotion was about when a shadow caught my attention.

"Is someone there?" I asked.

A barely audible voice said, "Please Ma'am, can you hold your dog? I'd like to talk to you."

I peered through the wrought iron gate and saw a fragile looking girl standing there.

"Who are you and what can I do for you?" I asked.

"I'm looking for work, Ma'am," she replied.

"Work? What kind of work do you have in mind?"

"Domestic work, Ma'am. I can clean and I'm a very good cook."

"I don't need any help. I have someone who comes in five days a week. She helps me with my cooking and laundry. And another woman comes twice a week to help with the heavy cleaning."

"I will only work for food. You don't have to pay me."

Tears came rolling down her cheeks and Flossy, who is usually vicious with strangers, kept looking at me with those pitiful eyes. He did that every time he wanted a treat. This young woman was looking at me with those same pleading eyes.

"Do you expect me to invite you, a complete stranger, into my house?" I asked her.

"No Ma'am, I don't."

For a split second I thought she was going to faint. "When was the last time you ate? You look hungry."

She hesitated for a moment and said, "Yesterday."

I remembered in the days when we had little to eat, my father once said to my mother, "If a stranger comes to your door, never ever turn him or her away, especially if they ask for food. It's a big sin. You do without a meal if you have to, but feed that hungry person."

I thought of all the food I had in the refrigerator and all the food I throw away every day. So, I opened the gate and invited her in. I felt that she was telling me the truth.

I thought Flossy would snap at her, but he kept walking behind us and wagging his tail as though he approved.

As we were walking up the stairs I said to her, "Look, young lady, I'll give you something to eat but if you are up to any tricks you can forget it. Just one word from me and this dog will tear you to pieces."

As we were walking up the stairs she said to me, "Ma'am, are you suffering from arthritis? Let me hold your hand."

"I'm OK," I said, "I just have to walk slowly."

When we got into the kitchen, I offered her a seat and made her two sandwiches. I also gave her some leftover chicken salad that was in the refrigerator.

Never had I seen anyone eat so fast. She ate one sandwich and the chicken salad and put the other sandwich aside.

"Don't you like cheese sandwiches?" I asked.

"Cheese sandwiches are my favorite, but I'm taking this one for my friends." She then took a serviette from the table and wrapped it up. She asked for a glass of water, but I gave her a Coke instead.

"Why aren't you working?" I asked. "A pretty young girl like you should have no difficulty finding a job!"

"Oh, how I wish I could find work," she replied. "But no one would employ me because I am here in Canada only on a visitor's visa. It cost me to get that visa and plane ticket."

"Where have you come from?"

"Guyana. The two girls with whom I'm staying, Sita and Rita, invited me to Canada. They said that jobs were plentiful and I would have no problem in finding work. I had worked at the Royal Bank in Guyana and they convinced me that since I had experience I would find a job in any one of the banks. My friends also assured me that if I did not find employment with any of the banks, that there are lots of other jobs available. Jobs where I could make some quick money. Unfortunately, they failed to tell me what I had to do to make money."

She paused, and when I said nothing, she went on, "I was brought up by my grandmother, who is a decent and honest person. After receiving several letters from my friends, I begged her to let me come to Canada, but she wouldn't agree. When I continued to beg and insist, she reluctantly agreed and gave me her blessing. 'Okay,' she said. 'Go to Canada. Get it out of your system. I know it was always your desire to see snow. Well go and see all the snow you want to, spend a few months and return. I'll be sitting right in this rocking chair waiting for you.'"

Her eyes softened and teared up. "My grandmother always sat in her favourite chair next to the window. If she were to see me now she would die from a heart attack. You could never imagine what it took for me to come to your door and beg for food. I have lost my dignity. I feel like a common beggar.

"For the past two weeks I have walked for several hours up-and-down Mississauga Road. I have seen you sitting in the garden a couple of times. Twice I came to the gate but I was scared. I didn't have the courage to approach you. But because I was hungry today, I took the chance to speak to you and to ask for your mercy."

"Why don't you return home?" I asked.

"Oh, I was determined to return home just a couple of days after I arrived. But it isn't very easy to get a flight to Guyana. And Sita and Rita said to me 'think of all the money you spent on your visa and the airline ticket. Almost ten thousand dollars. We know you are homesick and life is so different in Canada. But give yourself some more time to adjust.' To be honest all my life I dreamt of seeing the snow, and I did not want to return home without fulfilling my dreams."

"Believe me," I laughed, "after the first snowfall and a really cold day, you would wish that you had the warm weather of Guyana."

"I think there is someone at the gate," she said.

"Please God," I prayed. "Don't let it be any of my friends." My prayers were answered. It was only the postman with a registered letter for me to sign.

After signing the letter, it dawned on me that I had left her alone in my house. When I returned to the kitchen I saw that she had not only washed the plate and glass she had used, she had washed all my breakfast dishes that were lying in the sink.

"You didn't have to do that," I said. "I usually put them in the dishwasher."

"For only a few dishes?" she asked. "No need to."

She picked up the sandwich that she had wrapped, looked at her watch and said, "I have to go now. I usually do all the cooking when there is food in the house. The girls sleep most of the day."

As she was going through the kitchen door, she asked, "May I come and see you tomorrow? You are the kindest person I have met since I came to Canada."

She didn't wait for the reply. She looked at her watch once again and hurried down the stairs. I expected Flossy to run after her, but he didn't move. He lay on the floor wagging his tail.

I slept badly that night and woke up the next morning with a splitting headache. I slowly dragged myself to the medicine cabinet in my bathroom, looking for some aspirin, but apparently I had left the bottle in the kitchen cupboard when I had last used it. Throwing my housecoat over my nightgown, I headed straight for the kitchen.

"What's with that dog so early?" Flossy was barking and shaking the gate.

Probably it was the kids on their way to school. They teased Flossy all the time and he would snap at them. I went towards an open window in the living room and looked through it but I saw nothing out of the ordinary. But Flossy kept on barking. I opened the window as far as possible and pushed my head through. Lo and behold, I saw the girl from yesterday crouching at the gate. I hoped that David had not seen her on his way to work. Not even bothering to put on my slippers, I went through the front door and down the stairs. I was prepared to send her away and to tell her not to be a nuisance to me, but I couldn't. It was quite a cold morning and she was shivering. She was wearing the same summer dress she wore the day before.

"Now, come upstairs with me. I'm only doing this because I know you are freezing. I'll give you some breakfast, and you must leave immediately afterwards. And please, I don't want to see you hanging around my place anymore. Do you understand me?"

"Yes," she replied, then bowed her head.

As we were climbing the stairs, I stumbled and almost fell. She was walking behind me so she grabbed me, held onto me, and saved me from falling.

As I steadied myself, I said to her, "If I put too much weight on my right leg it tends to give way and I fall. I have severe arthritis and it is especially painful in the morning."

She kept holding my hand and as we reached the kitchen, she asked, "Where are your pills?"

"What pills?"

"Your arthritis pills, you didn't take them this morning, did you?"

I pointed to the cupboard above the sink. "My pills are in there. And see if there is a bottle of aspirin there also."

She found both my arthritis pills and the aspirin and handed the bottles to me. Then she took a bottle of water from the refrigerator and poured me a glass.

After I took the pills, she said, "Now you sit and relax, I'll make you some breakfast." From the refrigerator she took out a couple of eggs and asked me how I would like them prepared.

"Sunnyside up," I said, "and take out another couple for yourself."

"One is good enough for me," she replied. She cooked the eggs and made us some toast.

David always made a huge pot of coffee in the morning. He would usually drink a cup and read the newspapers before leaving for work. There was still plenty of hot coffee in the percolator, and the girl poured us both a cup. For a while we ate in silence and then I asked her why she was at my gate so early.

"It isn't so easy for me to explain."

"Try me."

"Where I am staying, sometimes over a dozen people come and stay overnight. Boys and girls. It's a very small townhouse. They smoke marijuana and sell drugs. People are in and out of the house all night long. Most of the time the bedrooms are occupied so I end up sleeping in the kitchen. By morning the house smells terrible and it is difficult to stay inside, so I leave the house as early as I can to breathe some fresh air.

"That sort of life scares me, but I know no one else in Canada so I have no place else to go. Two days ago, I was down, I was crying. But my grandmother's words kept coming back to me again. She said this to me and anyone else who spoke to her about their problems: 'Leave everything to God. Let him make the decision and something good is sure to happen.' I know I have been a complete nuisance to you, and it isn't easy for you to take a complete stranger from the street, someone who could be a thief and a liar, and bring them into your home. All I am asking you for is a place to stay and something to eat. I don't want a single penny from you. You have a room downstairs. I can clean it and stay there."

"Oh, no," I replied. "You can't stay there. It is my gardener's room. He stays there sometimes."

I paused for a moment, then looked at the girl. "One question, answer me honestly. Why can't your friends all find decent jobs?"

"Some of them I believe would like to. But they're mostly illegal immigrants."

"How did they get into the country?" I asked.

"Most of them paid for the visa like I did and they never returned to Guyana. A couple of them had really bad experiences when they worked in homes. One of the girls worked for a while at one of those homes at the other end of Mississauga Road. She worked from six in the morning to midnight. She looked after three small children and did some of the cooking and cleaning as well. She said her employer was a heartless devil and when things got unbearable, she went into work one day and told her employer that immigration had caught up with her and if she did not leave immediately she would be deported to Guyana and would never be able to return.

"Her employer paid her under the table and refused to pay her for the last month she worked. That did it. No one else ever tried to find a decent job again.

"Some of the people who come to the house are from New York. They are the ones who bring the drugs into the country. They have friends at the border.

"Also there is a Guyanese woman who runs a bus tour to the casino on the American side. Sometimes a few people would go on the bus to the casino. They pretend to go gambling and their friends would come in from New York and hand over the drugs to them. On their way back if a customs officer comes on the bus, everyone will say that they have lost the money at the casino. Most of the time it is true. So the ones who bring back the drugs return to Canada without any problem. They then hand over some money to the woman who runs the bus tour and she carries another set of them on the next bus tour she runs.

"When they came to the house last night I was so scared. I'm afraid that if the police raid the house, I will get thrown in jail with the rest of them. I don't want that to happen to me."

She began to cry and I felt dreadful. All she was asking from me was a chance to live a decent life. I didn't even know her name.

"What's your name?" I asked.

"Arshana."

"Arshana is a pretty name. Did I pronounce it correctly?"

"Yes, Ma'am."

"Arshana, you told me that you have been watching my house. Then you would've realized I do not live here alone, my son lives here with me and you would probably have noticed that I have visitors here all the time. What would I tell them if they were to come in and find you here?"

"Tell them, I'm a maid from one of the cleaning services. You have been using maid services? Haven't you?"

"You have been doing your homework on me, Arshana, and you seem to have a good answer for everything, but trust me, someone just has to look at you to know that you are not a maid."

I thought to myself, should I try her out? I really needed someone. Betty, my maid who had been with me for more than 15 years had gone back to Newfoundland to get married. She had helped with the cooking and did the laundry and dusting. Gladys came twice a week and did the heavy cleaning. But I knew I had to get someone to replace Betty.

"Look Arshana," I said. "Believe me, I want to help you but it is a very hard decision for me to make. Give me some time to think. My son is going away for a couple of weeks. He leaves on Sunday. After he's gone we will try and work something out. So in the meantime I beg you and implore you, just stay away from my gate."

"As you wish, Ma'am," she said.

I could see tears welling up in her eyes. She then bent her head and walked away like a wounded animal.

After that, I kept asking myself the same question over and over again. What should I do? I felt sorry for this young woman. I remembered how frightened and desperate my mother and I were when my father died; but we were fortunate enough to find someone who came to our assistance. Now I believed it was my turn to give something back.

Both my parents were survivors of the Holocaust. They met and married in Canada. My mother could not forget the ordeal she went through and spent most of her time in bed crying. On the other hand, my father worked at any job he could find to put food on our table. Jobs were very difficult to find in those days and after a while my father found steady work in a bakery. My father baked hundreds and hundreds of bagels and on Fridays he would go into the office and help Mr. Weissman, the store owner, with his accounts. My father was an accountant in the old country and Mr. Weissman was pleased with the way my father handled the books.

Eventually my father stopped baking bagels and worked fulltime in the office. Mr. Weissman gave my dad more and more responsibility and even a small raise. And then one day my father came home looking very sad. We learnt that Mr. Weissman had got into a heated argument with one of his employees and suffered a mild heart attack. Mr. Weissman was told not to return to the office and my father was more or less left in charge of the business. Mr. Weissman's son Solomon who had done one year in university had to drop out and take over the family business. My father showed young Mr. Weissman the tricks of the trade and everything went smoothly for a while. I also worked in the office on Saturdays and Sundays, which gave me a bit of pocket money. I saved every penny I earned for college and then one day my whole world came crashing down when my dad suffered a stroke in his office. He had high blood pressure and did not want to spend money on medication. "One sick person in the family is enough," he would tell me.

My father gave up living the day he had the stroke. He died due to complications a month later. Needless to say, my mother took to her bed permanently. She ate very little, spoke very little and cried all the time. I spent most of my days and a good part of the night holding her hand. I was devastated. I knew my dreams of going to college were over.

A couple of weeks after my father's funeral, the senior Mr. Weissman phoned and asked me to come down to his office. He only came to the office if it was really necessary. When he saw me he said, "Ruth, your father was one of the most honest men I have ever known. He wouldn't even take a bagel unless it was offered to him. I know you worked on weekends but your father was the only breadwinner in your family. But Ruth, I am prepared to offer you his job."

"Thank you, Mr. Weissman," I said. "But I don't think I could handle the responsibility."

"Yes, you could," Mr. Weissman said. "You speak good English, you are bright and no doubt you would learn quickly. Your father always boasted that you were a straight-A student. You wouldn't want to disappoint him, would you? I believe you have met my son, Solomon. He's also in the office and if there's anything you don't know or don't understand, ask him."

Solomon made sure that he gave me the desk next to his, and every so often I would catch him staring at me. On the days I worked late, he worked late also, and would offer me a lift home.

Many times, I would refuse and would tell him that it was out of his way, but he would insist and say that it was barely 10 minutes of his time and he didn't think a pretty girl should be riding the bus alone at night. Quite often if he did not have to be at home to have dinner with his parents, he would buy me a pizza or some chicken and come up to my parents' house and have dinner with us. My mother enjoyed his visits. He made her laugh and as soon as he left, she would say to me, "Ruth, that young man is interested in you. If he ever asks you to marry him, grab the opportunity."

"Mom, stop dreaming," I would say to her. "Mr. Weissman's parents would not want him to marry a penniless girl like me but a rich one. Every day many rich and beautiful girls came into the bakery and they come up into the office. Lots of them did not come to buy bagels."

"That might be so," my mother would say. "But take my word, that young man loves you and he will marry you someday."

My mother apparently knew what she was talking about, and it was too bad that she never found out. She died six months after my father.

At the funeral, Solomon said to me, "Ruth, there are so many wolves out there. I don't want you to be left alone. After you have taken the time you need to mourn, I'm going to marry you."

Solomon turned out to be a kind and generous husband. I wasn't madly in love with him when I married him, but with each passing day, I learned to love him more and more. I grieved a lot with his passing, but with David at my side, I was able to overcome my grief and adjust to life without Solomon.

The day came for David's trip. He and I sat in the living room waiting for his cab to arrive. He along with a couple of other doctors were going to Bermuda to play golf for a couple of weeks.

"Anything planned for the two weeks I'm away?" he asked.

I said casually, "Well David, do you remember my friend Eleanor who I volunteered with at the hospital?"

"I remember her, she's the one with the pretty daughter. I remembered it was either Cynthia or Ramona that said something to her and I never saw her again. What is she doing these days? What was her name again?" he asked.

"Gina," I said. "She's married to a Frenchman now and lives in Paris. She is expecting her first baby and Eleanor is going over to Paris to be with her for a couple of weeks. Anyways, Eleanor phoned yesterday to tell me that she was in a real predicament. Apparently, she has a house guest from Guyana and this girl or woman, whoever she is, knows no one in the country. So, Eleanor has asked me, or I should say begged me, to house her guest until she returns.

"I told Eleanor that I would be going on holidays in less than three weeks and she would have to return before that. Eleanor agreed to this because she has a return flight in two weeks. I then told Eleanor that I wasn't going to make any commitment until I see and speak to the person. She's bringing her here tomorrow."

David nodded, not noticing anything unusual about my story. "Here's my cab," he said.

David picked up his bag, kissed me goodbye and ran down the stairs before I could even say "have a nice trip."

2

Two weeks went by so quickly that I had almost forgotten that David was due to arrive that day. I was so involved in watching Arshana prepare dinner that I did not know he had arrived until I heard his familiar footsteps striding up the hall.

He dropped his bag as he entered the kitchen, looked at me, and then at René and then at Arshana.

"Am I in the right house?" he asked.

He looked rested and tanned but kept looking at me for an explanation.

"Oh, this is Arshana," I said introducing them.

"How was your flight?" I asked.

"I'll tell you all about my flight and my trip but just let me take my bags to my room and I will return in less than 10 minutes for a cup of tea."

I went to the living room to wait for him. I knew I was going to have to answer lots of questions.

He returned in less than 10 minutes and before he even sat down he asked, "Who is she?"

"David, do you remember before you left for Bermuda I told you that Eleanor had asked me to keep her house guest. Arshana is that guest."

"Is she staying here in this house?" he asked.

"It's a long story, David."

"Tell me, I'm not going anywhere. I have plenty of time."

"Well as you are probably aware, since Betty left I have tried several agencies and I was not pleased with the house help they sent me. But since this young woman has come I am pleased with everything she does. She even tries to help Gladys. And to crown it all she's a fantastic cook. She makes every kind of dish you can imagine. I wasn't sure what I should do with her.

"And then last week René and I were in the garden and she called us up for lunch. When I was climbing the stairs, I tripped and fell and almost broke my ankle. I was going to call Dr. Fine but both Arshana and René helped me to my room and got me to lie down.

"They wrapped my ankle with some kind of concoction and it helped the pain for a while. But at night the pain became unbearable. I took some painkillers and Arshana rubbed and soothed my ankle until I fell asleep. Apparently, she stayed with me all night, because when I woke up the next morning, she was curled up on the chair in my room fast asleep."

"How long is she going to be here?" he asked.

"I don't know David. I had a call from Eleanor a few days ago. She said Gina had lost her baby and there were complications. She asked me if l could keep her guest for a little while longer. She said she realized it was a big imposition on me but she said she couldn't leave Gina in her present condition."

"Has Auntie Sarah or Auntie Martha met her?"

"No, they haven't. I told them that I had hurt my ankle and I did not want visitors."

A smile touched his lips and I could see the twinkle in his eyes. The twinkle I noticed as a boy when he was mischievous.

Just then, Arshana entered with the tea tray.

"Oh, you should have told me that the tea was ready," I said to Arshana.

"It's all right," she said placing the tea tray on the nearby table. She had also bought us some of the cake she had baked the day before. "Shall I pour the tea?" she asked.

"No, I'll do it," David said.

As he poured the tea, he began to laugh.

"What is so funny?" I asked.

"I just can't wait to see the faces of Auntie Sarah and Auntie Martha when they meet your little helper."

"You won't have to wait much longer, David. They have just turned into the driveway."

David opened the door for them and as they walked into the living room, Martha said to David, "I thought you were in Bermuda."

"I returned just an hour ago and I am enjoying a cup of tea with Mom. Would you ladies care to join us or would you prefer a drink?"

"I'll have a drink later, but I would prefer a cup of tea right now," Martha said.

"Same here," Sarah said.

I left David chatting with them and I went to the kitchen to make a fresh pot of tea.

When I went to the kitchen, Arshana said to me, "You go and visit with your friends. I'll bring the tea."

When I returned to the living room, Sarah said to me, "I thought you were going to bring us some tea."

"The water is still boiling," I replied.

Just then Arshana appeared with the tea and two extra cups.

As she was about to pull the tea, David said to her, "Leave it, I'll do it."

Martha and Sarah stared at Arshana and then at me and then at David.

"Ruth," Sarah said, "Who is this girl?"

"Oh, I forgot," I said, like it was nothing. "I don't believe that either of you have met Arshana before?"

"I--how could we? Every time we try to visit you, you come up with some strange excuse. Didn't you want us to meet her, Ruth?" Sarah asked. "Are you hiding something?"

"Hiding what?" I asked. "It's a long story."

"David bring me that drink now," Sarah said.

"One for me too," Martha said. "And you better make it a double. I want to brace myself so I can hear this long story from your mother."

Arshana, who was still standing, took up the teapot and asked if she should refill it.

"That would be fine dear," I said.

As soon as Arshana returned to the kitchen, Sarah said, "Ruth we're listening. Who is she?"

"Well," I said. "You remember my friend Eleanor? Arshana was staying with her. And suddenly Eleanor had to leave for Paris she asked me if I could keep her guest until she returns. Arshana is from Guyana. She has only been in the country for about three weeks now. She's on holidays and she knows no one else in Toronto so she is staying with me until Eleanor returns.

"To be honest I'm enjoying her stay here with me and I hope Eleanor would stay away a little longer. I don't know what I would have done without her. She was a godsend when I twisted my ankle."

"Who is this Eleanor?" Martha asked

"Don't you remember her?" Sarah said. "The woman with a face like a horse."

David brought them their drinks and sat enjoying the little scene.

David wanted to irritate them a little more, so he said, "Eleanor might have a face like a horse, but if I remember correctly she has a beautiful daughter. What's the girl's name, Mom? Gina?"

"Oh yes, Gina," said Sarah. "Ramona and Cynthia fought with her all the time."

"She's now married to a rich and handsome Frenchman and lives in Paris."

"What happens if Eleanor does not return soon?" Martha asked. Then out of the blue she said to David, "Your mother needs to see a doctor. She has not been herself lately."

"I know she felt ill and fell and hurt her ankle when I was away, but I was not aware of any other medical problems," said David. Then turning to me he said, "I could always get Nancy to come over and see you tomorrow. She never listens to my diagnosis."

"David, I am perfectly healthy," I said.

"Ruth, I know it has been hard on you since Betty left, but all you have to do is call any one of these recognized agencies. They often supply excellent maid services," said Sarah.

"I don't think so, Sarah. Are you pleased with some of these agencies you have used? You have changed three maids in six months. I have no intention of looking for anyone just yet. I intend to keep Arshana until Eleanor returns. And by the way, she's not a maid. I do not think of her as a maid. She is educated and a very polite young woman. Apparently very well brought up and very respectful."

"Ruth," Martha said. "I hope you know what you are doing. That girl is far too attractive to be hanging around your house. I hope you will never have to regret it. You know what I'm drawing at. I certainly don't have to spell it out to you."

I knew what she was drawing at all night. Both Martha and Sarah were thinking about their daughters. David was not only an extremely successful doctor, but he was rich and handsome and a highly sought-after matrimonial catch. They were scared that their daughters might have some competition.

"David," Sarah said. "You are very wise and always fair with your judgment. We all respect your opinion. Do you honestly believe this cock and bull story that this girl has just arrived from Guyana and didn't know her way around? As you yourself said, Ruth, this girl is not stupid. She knows her way around all right. David, I don't want to hear anything from your mother. I want your honest opinion right now."

"Sorry, Auntie Sarah," David said. "At the moment I prefer to stay out of this. As you know I have just returned home, I don't know what the heck is going on. But I promise you soon as I find out, you can depend on me. I will give you my opinion."

"David," Martha said, "I need another scotch."

"And one for me too," Sarah said.

"I think you both have had enough already," David said. "I will give you both a small drink and no more. You don't want to be picked up by the police."

"Don't you remember? Our husbands are lawyers," said Martha.

"I am not thinking of you both going to jail," David replied. "My concern is if you kill some innocent person on the road home."

"Okay, doctor," Martha said. And to Sarah she said, "Finish your drink and let's go. David is saving his scotch."

They emptied their glasses. Without saying goodbye, they hurried through the door.

3

My waking and sleeping times were so mixed up that I woke up fuzzy headed after a night of terrible nightmares. I then went to the bathroom and splashed some cold water on my face. I got food and meditated afterwards. Any doubts in my head were dispelled. I decided I was going to listen to no one, and I was prepared to let Arshana stay with me as long as she wanted to stay.

The smell of fresh brewed coffee made me feel even better, so I hurried down to the kitchen.

David was already eating breakfast. When he saw me, he got up and pulled out a chair for me.

"Had a good night's sleep, Mom?" he asked.

"I wouldn't say so. I twisted and turned for hours before I fell asleep."

"What would you like for breakfast?" Arshana asked me.

David seemed to be enjoying his breakfast. "What is he eating?" I asked.

"Eggs," David said. "But there is a tiny problem. Can this young lady speak? She hasn't spoken a word to me or even answered any of my questions."

"Have you been teasing her, David?" I asked.

"No, I swear. I wasn't. Ask her."

Arshana did not answer. She just lowered her eyes, displaying long lashes against flushed cheeks.

David looked at his watch and said, "Good gracious me. I have been out of the office for two weeks and I'm running late. I should have been in my office half an hour ago."

"Will you be home for dinner?" I asked.

"I doubt it, but I will phone," he said. "I did promise to get togeth-er with the people I went to Bermuda with."

When he left I finished my breakfast and sat and watched Arsha-na as she did the dishes.

"Tell me about Guyana," I asked her.

"There isn't too much to tell right now. Everyone is trying to get out of Guyana because of the political unrest and corruption. As a mat-ter of fact, half of the people from Guyana are either here in Canada or in the United States. Lots of others would like to come here, but they can't afford to buy a visa to get out of the country."

"One of the young ladies who works at the salon where I do my hair says that Guyana is such a beautiful place," I said.

"Oh yes, it was. My grandmother often told me how good it was in the old days. People lived side-by-side happily, no matter their colour or race. All over the world, Guyanese people were known for their hos-pitality. But things have changed so much that very few people ever visit there anymore. Occasionally you may run into a few tourists, but they go mostly to see the Kaieteur Falls. Do you know that we have one of the highest waterfalls in the world in Guyana?"

"No, I didn't know that. In fact, I don't think I ever heard of the Kaieteur Falls," I said. "Where did you live? In the city or the country?"

"Oh, I lived just outside Georgetown, which is the capital. I come from a place called Kitty which is just outside the city. Like Mississauga to Toronto. I didn't know my parents. They both died when I was a baby and I was brought up by my maternal grandmother. Actually, she took care of me from the very day I was born. I am ashamed to say that I have cried every night for her since coming to Canada. I should have listened to her when she told me not to come to Canada. And now I'm paying the price for disobeying her."

"Is Guyana far from Trinidad?" I asked.

"Less than an hour by plane," she said.

"The two ladies who visit here have had maids from Guyana too. Sati, that was Sarah's maid, was deported after she was caught shoplifting and Shanti, Martha's maid, married someone so she could stay on in Canada. They were both illegal immigrants.

"Every year my friends and I choose some exotic place to visit. Last year we almost went to Trinidad, but at the last moment we changed our minds and went to Singapore instead.

"What time is it now? Oh dear me, they should be here any time now I said. I'll see if I can convince them to go to Trinidad and Guyana."

"Maybe they have arrived," Arshana said. I could hear Flossy barking. René was in the garden, he would open the gate for them.

A few moments later both Sarah and Martha came flying up the hall. "We chose to come through the back door," Sarah said, "We smelt something good cooking in the kitchen."

"I was just finishing breakfast," I said. "There is plenty of coffee in the pot, would you girls like some?"

Arshana did not wait for their reply. She took down two mugs from the cupboard and poured them some coffee.

"What is your maid, or help, or whatever you want to call her, cooking?"

"Sarah," I said. "I'd appreciate if you would stop being sarcastic about Arshana. She's a guest in my house and she will stay here as long as Eleanor is away. So, you better get used to seeing her around."

"Look you two," Martha said. "I have not come here to fight. I have come to talk about our vacation. Choose a place, someone."

"I have been learning so much about Guyana and Trinidad from Arshana that I would like to go there. And we could be certain of one thing: it would be hot there," I said.

"Shanti did mention that there are beautiful beaches in Trinidad," said Martha. "I don't believe she said anything about beaches in Guyana, but there are other things you can do to occupy your time for a couple of days. She also said that if you want nice gold jewelry, Guyana is the place to buy it."

"Sarah," Martha said. "Finish your coffee. Let's go right now to the travel agency. As far as I remember, Venezuela is quite close to Trinidad and we could even make a quick trip there. We'll let you know what we find out, Ruth."

Sarah said, "I'll call you after dinner. In the meantime, enjoy your guest and her cooking."

"I certainly will," I said, closing the back door behind them.

4

"Here's a copy of this morning's paper," René said as he handed it to me. As I was browsing through the pages I found a flyer that said there was a huge end of summer sale at Sherway Gardens.

"René," I said, "see what that girl is doing in the kitchen. Tell her to finish up what she's doing and that we're going shopping."

"I don't like shopping, Ma'am," Arshana called out quickly from the kitchen.

"What young girl doesn't like shopping?" And then it hit me she probably had no money. She had been with me for three weeks and I had not paid her a penny. Having to tell so many lies and evade all the different questions about her, it never crossed my mind to ask her about money.

"Arshana," I said, walking into the kitchen. "Have you got any money?"

"What do I need money for?" she asked. "You give me a place to stay and food to eat. What more do I need? And when I came and begged you for work, we agreed on what my terms were, and I have received from you more than I need."

"Arshana, please tell me how much money you have in your possession right now."

"I don't have any money at the moment. I did have some money saved up for an emergency, but when I visited my friends a couple of days ago, they were behind on their rent and about to be evicted, so I gave the money I had saved to them. In a few days my grandmother will be sending me money, so I will have money."

I opened my purse, took out five hundred dollars and handed it to her. "Take this," I said, "And as long as you are staying and helping out in my house, I will be paying you every week."

She refused to take the money and lowered her head.

"Arshana, if you don't take this money, then I can't let you stay here anymore. I know there's always ample supplies of toiletries in all my rooms. But it never occurred to me that you might need other necessities. I will not allow you to work for me for free. And if there's anything else you need, I want you to ask me. Do you understand?"

She reluctantly took the money, put it in her purse and said "thank you."

"Now I'm going downstairs to have a word with René, meet us in 10 minutes by the front gate."

She met me at the gate and René said, "Miss Arshana looks sad."

As the three of us got into the car, I said to René, "She doesn't want to go shopping."

"Are we going very far?" Arshana asked as we pulled out of the driveway.

"Not very far," I said. But the traffic was heavy and when we did arrive at Sherway Gardens there was not a single parking spot inside. We drove around and around for about 10 minutes and then we got lucky, someone pulled out not too far from the main entrance and we drove into the spot. As we parked she said, "I've never seen such huge a place before. So many cars and so many people."

"Oh, you just wait till you get into the mall," I said.

I was right. The mall was so crowded that people kept bumping into each other. The following Tuesday was back to school for the kids. So parents were trying to do some last-minute shopping.

We browsed several shops and then I heard someone calling my name. It was Monique. She owned a boutique in the mall and I had purchased several dresses from her in the past.

"Haven't seen you for a while, Mrs. Weissman," she said as we entered the boutique. "You should have been here sooner. The sale started three days ago and all my best dresses are sold out. But look around, you might still find something that pleases you."

Arshana was walking behind me and when Monique saw her, she turned to me and said, "If this young lady is with you, Mrs. Weissman, I have a few beautiful dresses left in her size. She's petite and they don't go so fast."

"I didn't need any dresses," Arshana said.

"Don't listen to her, Monique," I said. "Show us some of your dresses."

Monique went to the back of the store and returned with two dresses. One was an emerald green cocktail dress. The other just a plain red dress. "These dresses are exactly your size, young lady," Monique said. "The colors are just perfect for your skin tone. Even if you don't like them, try them on and let me see how they look on you."

Arshana looked at the price tags and refused to try them on.

"Arshana, I insist that you go into the fitting room and try on the dresses," I said.

Reluctantly she went into the fitting room and came out in less than five minutes, saying that they did not fit.

"Arshana," I said. "I don't believe you tried on those dresses. Please put them on. I want to see if they fit."

I handed her the emerald green dress, gave her time to put it on and then went into the fitting room.

Both Monique and I were amazed at how beautiful she looked in the dress.

"I'll have that dress," I said to Monique. And to Arshana I said, "Put the red dress on."

The red dress was just perfect for her slim figure so I said to Monique, "Wrap them up." After I paid Monique and we were about to leave, she said to me "Mrs. Weissman, believe me, I am not looking for more sales, but I have a beautiful peacock dress that is made for this young lady. On a second thought, I think it is sold out, but let me take a look at the back."

Monique returned with the dress and said, "If this dress fits the young lady, take it for half the price."

The dress fitted Arshana perfectly and I took it.

After I paid for the dresses and was leaving the store, Monique said to me, "Mrs. Weissman, three doors away is a newly opened shoe shop. They sell all kinds of sandals. You will find some beautiful golden sandals that would go well with all these dresses. I couldn't get my size but I don't think you would have any problem in finding a pair to fit her."

She was right. We found a beautiful pair of open-toed sandals. Hanging on the wall was a gold mesh bag. I bought them both.

The mall got more and more crowded. There was absolutely nowhere to sit. And thinking of buying lunch was almost impossible. You couldn't even get into a line at any of the food stalls, so we decided to buy lunch on the way home.

Just before we left the mall, I saw a beautiful coat on one of the store mannequins. It was an all-purpose coat and was made from white cashmere and wool.

"Come and try this on," I said to Arshana. "It will keep you warm until you leave in January."

When she hesitated I said, "You don't have a winter coat do you? This coat will fit you perfectly. This is one of your Christmas presents. Though you are going to have to use it long before Christmas."

"But you have not bought anything for yourself," she said.

"I really don't need anything. I have tons of clothes in my closet. Some of them still have price tags on. I am sure I will find something to wear on the trip."

On our way home, I asked her if she would like us to stop at Harvey's for a hamburger.

"Why spend more money," she said. "We have plenty of food in the fridge."

As we drove home, she sat quietly in the car.

"Have I said something to offend you?" I asked.

"It is wrong for me to accept your money, your gifts, your food and everything else you give me."

"We'll talk about that later," I said.

David's car was in the driveway, so I knew he was home already.

After we parked, she tried to collect all the packages. "Arshana," I said, "How many pairs of hands do you have?"

I took some of the packages from her and as we walked up the stairs David opened the door for us. He took some of the packages from us and asked if we had bought out the mall.

"Even if we wanted to, we couldn't have. We had to fight our way through the crowd to get these few items. We couldn't even find a place to have some lunch," I said.

"So, I believe that you ladies should be very hungry," he said. "My meeting was canceled so I could take you both out for dinner."

"I accept," I said. "This offer doesn't come my way too often."

"I'd rather not go," Arshana said.

"Why, do you have a date?" David asked.

"There is plenty of food in the fridge," she said.

"Well I don't like leftovers," David replied. "And now I am going to my room for a short nap. I'll be down here in the living room at six o'clock and I want to find you ladies here waiting for me? Understand?" He gave me a hug, pulled Arshana's hair and left.

By five-thirty I was ready. I went and knocked at Arshana's door and when she opened the door I saw that she was wearing one of the dresses she had brought from Guyana. "That's a pretty dress," I said, "But why don't you wear the green dress we bought today?"

"No, that dress is far too fancy for me," she said.

"Come on," I said. "The dress is very simple." I could see the red dress was still wrapped in tissue, lying in the box.

I took it out and handed it to her and said, "Put it on quickly. We don't want to keep the doctor waiting. When he says six o'clock he means five to six."

I left her to put the dress on and I joined David who was already in the living room. He was making himself a martini and had one ready for me.

At five to six, Arshana walked into the living room, her head bent, and she looked scared and nervous.

For a split second I did not recognize her. She looked so different. Her hair was always in a ponytail and most of the time she wore jeans. But her dress fit perfectly, displaying her slender waist and narrow hips. Her long dark hair fell loosely to her shoulders and the only jewelry she wore was a pendant I had often seen her wear.

"Want a drink before we go?" David asked her.

"No sir, I never drink alcohol," she replied.

"Do you believe her, Mom?" asked David.

"Yes, I do."

David took us to a famous little Italian restaurant, The Mona Lisa. The decor was simple except for the huge portrait of the Mona Lisa hanging on the wall. The tables were dimly lit with candles. A pianist was making beautiful music and singing in Italian. Several couples were dancing and a few of them were even singing along.

As soon as Gino the head waiter saw us, he came over to our table and said to David, "are you comfortable at this table or should I get you another one, sir?"

When David told him that our table was fine, Gino whispered something in David's ear. He then recommended the chef's special and handed us each a menu.

"Look over the menu, sir. Take your time. And should I bring you a bottle of your favorite wine?"

"Good idea, Gino."

As we were looking over our menus, Arshana whispered in my ear, "I can't believe the prices."

"What's all that whispering about?" David asked.

"Arshana thought that the prices are ridiculous and I'm inclined to agree with her."

"Too bad," David said. "If I can't afford to pay, the two of you will end up in the kitchen doing dishes."

Gino returned with the wine and three glasses. David insisted on pouring the wine himself, so he poured a glass for me and as he was about to pour one for Arshana, she said, "Sorry sir, I prefer a coke."

"Gino can get you a Coke, but I want you to stop calling me sir, it makes me uncomfortable." Then he turned to me and said, "Mom, doesn't she know my name?"

"David, I hope you have more success than me. I can't get her to stop calling me Ma'am."

"Listen young lady, my name is David and I would rather you call me by my name. And with regards to my mother you either call her Mrs. Weissman or Mom. Have I made myself clear? And by the way, do you know how to get home from here?"

"No," Arshana said, shaking her head.

"So, if you don't listen to what I just said," David told her. "You might have to walk home." I was just about to tell David to stop teasing her when a young woman walked over to our table.

"David," she said. "Do you know that I have been trying to get in touch with you for the past two weeks? I even went to your office earlier today and was told that you had already left. I wanted to know if you are accompanying us to the medical convention in California."

"I was all set to go, Barbara, but as you know I have just returned from Bermuda and found poor Dr. Fine in a mass confusion in the office. Not only was she stuck with my patients, but she had to deal with a lot of staff problems in the office. The woman is totally burnt out so I suggested she go to the convention and take a little holiday at the same time."

"Well David," said Barbara, "Do you know Dr. Nicole Jarvis?"

"Yes," David said, "She went to Bermuda with us."

"I saw her yesterday," Barbara continued, "And she said she now needs a holiday. Guess you are pretty burned out too. And I'm not talking about the sun."

"I'll phone you on Monday, Barbara," David said. "Gino is here to take our order."

"Thank you," Barbara said.

As Gino was about to take our order David said to him, "No tip for you tonight Gino. And maybe, before I leave, I'll strangle you."

"I didn't say a word to her, sir."

After we placed our order, I asked David whether there was anything wrong.

"Nothing," he said. And to Arshana, who was smiling, he asked, "What are you smiling about?"

"I always smile when I hear Nat King Cole's Mona Lisa."

"Since you like that song so much, you little fibber, come around and dance to it." He stretched out his hand and Arshana looked at me with pleading eyes.

"Can't help you," I said. "You know I have arthritis and can't walk the long distance home."

With so much responsibility in the office, David was always so tense, but he seemed relaxed when he danced with Arshana.

When they returned to the table, he said that Arshana's boyfriend did not only tell her not to drink alcohol, but that she should not dance with strange men either.

"It's not my boyfriend," Arshana replied. "It's my grandmother who wanted me to stay away from strangers."

"Did your grandmother ever see you on the dance floor?" David asked.

"Of course, she did."

"Mom, she knows how to dance. I believe she has been dancing all her life."

"We have fun in Guyana too," Arshana said demurely.

David teased her throughout dinner and after dinner, I said, "Okay, David, stop teasing her and ask Gino to bring the dessert trolley."

David made a sign to Gino and he swept over with the dessert trolley. Such a selection. I didn't know what I should try. There was fresh fruit, cheese and crackers and a variety of pastries.

"Look at the cheesecake," I pointed out to Arshana. "Try a slice. You love cheesecake."

"No thank you," she said.

"She never eats a good meal," I said to David. "But she loves cake and ice cream."

"Gino, give that young lady a piece of cheesecake," David said.

"I'll try a piece also," I said.

"Your usual coffee and liqueur, sir?" Gino asked David. "I know what you like, sir."

"Stop buttering me up, Gino," David said. "I'm definitely going to get you fired tonight."

"I swear sir, I swear on my mother's grave I didn't say a word. Dr. Barbara kept asking me who this young lady was and when I told her I didn't know, she didn't believe me. Now, I am in trouble all around."

"You don't know what trouble is," David said to Gino. "When I am through with you, you will find out what real trouble is. Now let's have some coffee."

"None for me," Arshana said. "Mom, have you seen the price for a cup of coffee? We can buy a bottle for that price."

"Well, that's a start," David said to me. "She called you Mom. I guess she is afraid to walk home."

Just then, the band which had been on a short break began to play. Someone requested Al Martino's Spanish Eyes as David said to Arshana, "Let's dance." Once again, she turned towards me for help, and I said to her, "I am far too full to walk home or do dishes."

Reluctantly she got up and they danced. After the dance, they returned to our table and we finished our coffee and liquor and headed home."

When we reached home, David said, "I don't know about you ladies but I had an enjoyable evening, so good night, and thank you both once again," and he went off to bed.

5

Sarah's husband, John, was born on the first of July and it was customary for Martha, Sarah, the kids and I to throw him a party. Even John and Sarah's son, Lyle, who was busy planning his own wedding, helped out. The party was usually held on the Saturday following the Canada Day celebrations. Since I have a huge party room with all the necessary conveniences, the party was always held at my place.

Every year John would say that he didn't want a party, but we all knew he looked forward to it. It gave him the opportunity to invite some of his closest friends from the office. On the night of the party, after I was finished dressing, I went to Arshana's room to see how she was getting along. But instead of finding her dressed, I found her sitting on her bed in tears.

"Why aren't you dressed? What's wrong?" I asked.

"I don't want to go to the party and I don't have to tell you why. I am looked down upon as the hired help and I don't think many people would appreciate my presence."

"Too bad for them," I said. "This is my house, Arshana, and if anyone should make any stupid comments to you, just ignore them and let me know right away. I am going downstairs now to see how things are shaping up, and when I return I want to see you wearing the peacock blue dress we bought the other day at Monique's."

Cynthia and Ramona did not need my help. They had everything organized already. The party was supposed to begin at 7 o'clock but it seemed that everyone was there already.

When Ramona saw me, she came over and said, "Auntie Ruth, we're all set. The bar is already open and I have instructed the caterers to put out the buffet around 8 o'clock."

We both turned as we heard stumbling footsteps. "Here comes Eric," Ramona said. "He seems to have had enough already. I bet he was drinking before he got here."

Eric was Martha's son, and there was no doubt that he was already drunk.

"Auntie Ruth, Auntie Ruth," Eric shouted. "Where's David? I haven't seen him around."

"He went out just after lunch and I have not seen him since. And Eric," I continued. "There are so many beautiful young women around, why don't you go and talk with them."

"I need a few more drinks to build up some courage."

"You don't need more drinks right now, Eric, you have already spilt half the drink in your hand. Now have a seat. I am going upstairs for a moment. If your parents happen to arrive before I return, tell them I'll be down shortly."

I went straight to Arshana's room and rapped on her door. As I opened the door, I saw her standing at the window, tears streaming down her cheeks.

"Now dry those tears quickly. I want to see how you look in your dress. Arshana, I have just come from downstairs and there's not one woman who looks as beautiful as you do. Now come on, let's go downstairs."

Martha and Sarah had arrived and they were sitting at a corner table. Martha nudged Sarah when she saw us, so I chose not to sit with them, but at another table adjoining theirs.

When Carl, Martha's husband saw us, he came over immediately and asked us what we would like to drink.

I said "A glass of white wine for me, thank you Carl, and the same for the young lady."

Before Carl could act on my request, Arshana said, "No thank you. I'd prefer a Coke."

"I'd like a drink too," Martha shouted. "Or haven't you noticed that I'm sitting here?"

"You already have a drink in your hand," Carl said to her.

"Not anymore," Martha replied as she emptied her glass. "And now I'd like you to fetch me a scotch and soda with very little ice."

"Anything for you, Martha," Carl said.

Eric, who had been watching us the whole time, came staggering to our table as soon as his father left. "I don't believe I have met this beautiful lady as yet, Auntie Ruth. Introduce me."

Before I could introduce him, I saw David and a young man walk in. They were headed straight in our direction.

Eric quickly turned to his mother and said, "Moolah, big moolah. That guy with David is Dr. Ken Campbell. Family is loaded. They donate millions of dollars to charity every year."

"Do you know him, Eric?" Martha asked.

He responded, "I have met him a couple of times. He is a very good friend of David's. He doesn't have to work but occasionally he works in David's clinic to keep up with the latest in medicine."

"Introduce him to Cynthia or Ramona," Martha said.

"Be quiet, Mom," Eric said. "They're coming to the table."

"This is my mom," David said as he introduced Ken Campbell to me. "Ken here is forever gallivanting around the globe. As a matter of fact, he is off to South America in a couple of days." And turning to Arshana, David told Ken, "This young lady is from South America."

"Good," Ken said. "I want to sit next to her."

Arshana bent her head and I knew she was embarrassed, so I said to Ken, "Please do sit with us."

"David," Sarah called out. "Aren't you supposed to kiss your aunt when you see her?"

"Just give me a few minutes. I'll run up, take a quick shower, and I'll return and kiss all the ladies." And to Ken, he said, "Keep the ladies happy."

In less than 20 minutes, David returned dressed in cream slacks and a dark blue silk shirt.

"Come here, David," I said to him. "I don't care how many doctors or lawyers or accountants are here tonight, you know no one is as handsome as you are."

"You are my mother and if you don't think so, who else will?" he replied. Then he turned to Ken and said, "How are you doing? Come and let me introduce you to some of the ladies around."

"To be honest David, I'm enjoying the company of this young lady," he said, referring to Arshana. "But I won't refuse if you were to take me to the bar."

And to Arshana, Ken said, "Hold on to my seat, I will be right back."

Ramona had chosen a complete entertainment package for the party. It included a regular and a seafood buffet, a band, a singer and a DJ. Just before 8 o'clock, Ramona came to me and asked if it was time to serve dinner. When I told her I believed so, she beckoned to the waiter to set up the buffet table. Everything you could imagine was on that table. Delicacies galore. Everyone started filling their plates. Ken went to the buffet table and returned with a plate of cold cuts and rolls.

"You just said that you like curry and roti, why didn't you get some?" Arshana asked, smiling.

"There was no curry and roti on the table. If there was curry and roti, do you think I would have had all this junk on my plate?" Ken asked, grinning conspiratorially.

"Mom," Arshana whispered to me. "There is no curry and roti on the buffet."

"Probably Cynthia or Ramona did not want it on the table. Let me ask them. Oh, there is one of the caterers, I will ask him."

I approached the waiter and said, "Did you not see some curry and roti in the kitchen?"

"Yes Mrs. Weissman," he replied. "I did, but with so many other dishes, I put the curry and roti in the oven to keep warm, and I completely forgot to put it out. Please, do forgive me. I'll put them on the table right away." Satisfied, I rejoined my table.

"I didn't see you go up to the buffet table," Ken was saying to Arshana. "Here," he said, "Take my plate, I'm going for curry and roti."

Arshana laughed and gently pushed away his plate.

Ken and John returned to our table, their plates filled with roti and curry. As they took their seats, Sarah, who was at the next table, came over and said to John sarcastically, "I think you need a bigger plate."

"We never have curry at home anymore," John said to her. "So if you don't mind, let me eat as much as I can here."

"Pig," Sarah said as she walked away. "And if you like curry that much, find a maid who can cook it."

"We had a maid, remember?" John said. "And you drove her away."

"Oh," Ken said to Arshana. "I better go and have another helping before it all disappears."

"Oh, there's lots," Arshana said. "And I don't believe that many people will eat curry."

But when Ken returned minutes later he said to Arshana, "I got news for you. The curry and roti disappeared. Both platters are empty."

"No more left?" John asked. "I was just going for some more."

"Out of luck, buddy," Ken said.

John said, "Ruth, you know how much I like curry and I am sure you had this young lady prepare it especially for me. Am I right?"

I thought about this and said "When you go out to dinner, John, where do you like to go?"

"To an Indian restaurant. But this young lady has made curry the way I like, not too spicy. We once had a maid from Trinidad and she made curry all the time. Similar to the one you made tonight."

"Is your curry different?" I asked Arshana.

"Almost the same as what you will find in the Indian restaurants, but in Guyana and Trinidad we tend to make our curries less spicy, so it isn't so hot and the flavour is a bit different."

"Ruth," said John. "Next Wednesday, I am not working late so I'll come straight from my office to your house for dinner."

"I am leaving the country on Thursday, but you can come for dinner on Wednesday."

"It's up to Arshana," I said. "If she's willing to cook, you gentlemen are certainly welcome."

"I'm your Uncle John," John said to Arshana. "And I'm sure you would make dinner for me. Won't you?"

Arshana did not reply, but just looked at John and smiled.

Eric was still sitting at the table next to ours, with his mother. He was grumbling and fussing.

"What's wrong, Eric?" I asked him, "Why don't you go upstairs and take a short nap on one of the couches?"

"I didn't come here to nap, Auntie Ruth. Where is the music? We paid tons of money for the band and the singer."

He called out to the band. The band took their positions and the singer went over to the mic and asked if there were any special requests. One couple requested 'Lady from Calcutta' and several couples got up and danced and sang along.

Eric got up from his seat, came to our table, grabbed Arshana's arm and said, "Lady from Guyana, let's dance."

"Please leave me," Arshana said, looking upset. And when he continued to grab at her, she pushed him away, and he staggered and fell.

"Who the hell do you think you are?" Eric shouted. He struggled to his feet and grabbed at Arshana again.

"Behave yourself, Eric!" I reacted.

Then Ken, furious at Eric, took hold of him and ground out, "I think you have had enough, buddy. Leave the lady alone."

David was standing at the bar and had just noticed the incident. He strode over to our table, but before he reached it, Ken took Arshana's hand and led her onto the dance floor.

"What's going on, Mom?" David asked.

"David, forget about it," I told him. "John and his friends are looking in our direction and poor Carl is so terribly embarrassed by his son's behaviour."

"Hi David," Ken said as he returned to our table. "I was just waiting to say goodbye."

David then walked him to the door.

"Ruth, are you blind?" Martha asked. "Can't you see what is happening? That girl is flirting with all the men here. She was flirting with Eric and then she tried to play innocent. She wanted Ken Campbell to come to her assistance. She couldn't care less about you or David. She's looking for bigger fish to catch. She knows all about Ken Campbell and his family's wealth. He was the only person she spoke to all this time."

Martha's voice was so loud that Arshana heard everything she said. Turning to me, Arshana said, "I hope you see my reason for not wanting to come. You insisted and I obeyed, but I am not going to take any more insults. I am going to my room."

John, who along with several others, had seen Eric's behavior, walked over to our table.

"Hello, young lady, to show my appreciation for that lovely curry, may I have the next dance?" John asked.

"I was just leaving," Arshana said. And she looked towards me with her pleading eyes.

"Go ahead and dance with Uncle John," said John, trying again.

"Ruth, do you see what I mean?" Martha said. "Even John, who is as cold as ice, is beginning to unfreeze."

"Martha, both you and Sarah have been rude and sarcastic all evening," I said firmly. "So if you don't mind, please hold your tongues. I am going to forgive you both, because you are drunk, but I am not prepared to listen to any more nonsense."

David, who was standing close by, heard all that I said, and from the expression on my face he knew I was mad.

"Everything OK, Mom?" he asked.

Before I had the chance to reply, Dr. Nancy Fine came over to our table and said she was leaving.

"But I didn't have a chance to dance with you," David said.

"How could you? You were too busy charming the blonde bimbos at the bar. And I guess you are tired of seeing this old bag in the office all day."

"Nancy, there is no one here tonight who could replace you in my heart. Come, let's dance."

"David, you are talking to Nancy Fine. You can pull the wool over those dumb bimbos, but remember I have been listening to your conversations for years. I can read you like a book. Now walk me to my car."

And as he put his arm around her, he said, "By the way, I have something to discuss with you, Nancy."

"I am not discussing business tonight, David. Just walk me to my car."

When he returned, David said to Arshana, who was just about to leave, "Let's dance."

Her dark eyes were unreadable and in a perfectly polite and casual way, she said, "If you don't mind, I'd rather not."

"Come on," David said. "Why worry with what other people may say or think? They're playing Save the Last Dance for Me and I would like to have this last dance with you."

Reluctantly, she got up and they began to dance. Suddenly everyone stopped dancing. There were loud screams of breaking glass. The bartender came rushing out of the bar and as he was about to walk through the door, he said to Ramona, "I am not paid enough for this abusive treatment."

Apparently, Eric had tried to punch him when he refused to give him another drink.

Poor Carl was so humiliated. He hung his head and walked over to Martha and said, "Take your drunk son home. He has embarrassed me in front of my co-workers."

Several guests became uncomfortable, and fearing that there might be further trouble, they slowly left the party.

"Mom, you and Arshana go upstairs and go to bed. René is still here. We'll put the lights out and see to everything," David said.

I didn't even bother to say goodnight to anyone. I just climbed the stairs and Arshana followed behind me. "Never, never again will I ever allow another party in this house," I promised. "Good night, Arshana." She went to her room and I went to mine.

6

I could hear René mumbling in Spanish. He always mumbled in Spanish when anything or anyone upset him. I put my head through the window and saw that he was potting some plants.

"It's too hot to be planting. Come on up and let's have some tea."

"One moment, Ma'am."

Five minutes later he appeared.

"What are you mumbling about, René?"

"It's that devil Mrs. Chopra. She is forever spying over here. A few minutes ago, I saw her peeping through a hole in the fence. And you know what I did? I picked up my hose and pretended that I was watering the new plants and squirted the water right in her eyes."

David, who was sitting by the window reading a book, said, "You shouldn't have done that René, you could have hurt Mrs. Chopra."

"It would have served her right, sir. She is always annoying me. Yesterday she shouted at me over the fence and said 'René, how are Mrs. Weissman's lawns always so immaculate, her shrubbery always nicely pruned and her flowers in the garden always blooming?'

"I told her 'If you want your garden to look like Mrs. Weissman's you'll have to spend money like Mrs. Weissman. She not only pays me well but spends lots of money on her garden.'

"Sir, that woman is not only cheap but mean and miserable. Mana, the cleaning lady, she left her yesterday after working for her less than a week. Mana said if Mrs. Chopra offered to pay her in gold, she'd never work for her again. She accused Mana of taking water, could you believe it? Just plain water from her refrigerator. Mana told me she didn't do it because Mrs. Chopra told her never to go into the fridge unless she was cleaning it. I believed Mana. For years, nearly ten years, I worked for Mrs. Chopra, and never once did she offer me a glass of water. In fact, I have never even been in her kitchen. Had it not been for Dr. Chopra, I would have quit a long time ago. Every time I told him that I was leaving, he begged me to stay.

"I know the hell that poor man is going through. I am going through it myself with that devil of a wife I have. I told Miss Arshana that I am planning to return to my old country. She begged me to stay until January. She says we could both leave together."

"By the way," René continued. "She has been gone a long time." He looked at his watch. "It has been more than an hour.

"Oh, there she is, running as usual," I said. I was looking out the window and saw Arshana running through the fields, her long hair flowing in the wind.

A few minutes later she came running up the front steps, almost out of breath, holding a small package in her hand.

"Sorry, I didn't mean to stay so long," she said to me.

"René was the one who was worried. Not me," I said jokingly.

"I was just going to make some iced tea," René said. "But I don't have the time. The other devil, my wife, is waiting for me at the mall and if I keep her waiting, she will chew my head off."

"I'll make the tea, René," Arshana said. "I want you to taste the cake I made yesterday. I made the one you like with lots of chocolate."

"Keep a piece for me. I'll eat it tomorrow," René said as he left.

Arshana went to make the tea, and David asked me, "Where does she go?"

"I don't know where to begin David, it's a long story. I have not been truthful with you or anyone else. Arshana was never a house guest at Eleanor's."

He took off his glasses, put his book down and said, "What is the truth, Mom? Start from the beginning, I have plenty of time to listen."

"David, you wouldn't want to know where she goes or who her friends are. They are prostitutes, drug addicts, illegal immigrants, and I believe some of them have even been to jail."

"Why does she associate with these people?"

"Arshana knows two of the girls from Guyana, Sita and Rita. They told her that there was lots of money to be made in Canada, but when Arshana arrived and saw how they were making their money, they convinced her that she had spent so much money on her airline ticket and visa that she should stay at least a couple of months and see a bit of Canada.

"Arshana lived in fear that something terrible would happen in that house full of drugs and alcohol and criminals, so when she couldn't take it anymore, she came straight here begging for help.

"I could see that she was a decent girl and well brought up, and knowing what I knew, I could not let her return to that house, David. René was at the gate and when he saw her, he held her and calmed her down by letting her rest in his room. They were both crying when I went down to his room.

"René said to me 'I'm going to take her to the British West Indies Airline office to see if she can get an earlier return ticket, so in the meantime Ma'am, I beg you, please let her stay.'

"This was around the time that you left for Bermuda and I thought that if she could get her flight changed, she may leave before you even returned, but she couldn't get an earlier flight. There was absolutely nothing available for a month."

"But why does she continue to go there?" David asked.

"Because the girls are her only connection to Guyana and the only people she knows in Canada. And also her mail is sent to that address."

"Is she here illegally?"

"No David, she's here on a visitor's visa. She's permitted to stay in Canada until January."

"But you are breaking the law by employing her."

"I'm not employing her. She is a friend who is staying with me until she leaves Canada. I don't have to pay her. If anyone cares to check, her grandmother sends her money all the time."

Before he could ask me any more questions the phone rang. It was one of the few times I was glad to hear Sarah's voice.

"Ruth, our trip is booked and confirmed and we leave on Saturday. It is a 21-day trip. We're booked for seventeen days in Trinidad because they have beautiful beaches there. We could spend the other four days in Caracas, or wherever else we want. We can look into that when we get there. Oh and Ruth, I'm not so sure if I mentioned it to you last week, but Joanne, Lyle's fiancé's mother, will be joining us on the trip."

"You never said a word to me, Sarah."

"Perhaps it was Martha I mentioned it to. Yes, it was Martha. She had no objection. In fact, she was delighted. Joanne has been in Trinidad and Venezuela a couple times, so we're lucky to have her as a guide.

"Joanne's daughter Jenny was twice divorced and had a couple of kids from each of her marriages. At first both John and Sarah objected to Lyle and Jenny's marriage, but in the end, they gave in, because Jenny's father Kirk was the most senior partner in the law firm where both John and Lyle worked.

"Ruth, before I forget, Martha and I were talking last night and we were concerned about that girl you have staying in your house."

"I'm glad you brought that up. No need for you both to be concerned. Arshana went back to Eleanor's and it has been so miserable around here since she left."

"Miserable? You should thank God. At least you can enjoy your holiday with peace of mind."

"She's a nice girl and I am sorry she had to go."

"Ruth Bunker!" Sarah always called me Ruth Bunker if I did not agree with them. She was referring to Archie Bunker's wife, Edith, from *All in the Family*. "Have you ever thought about David, Ruth?"

"Sarah, David treats her like any other girl."

"But that girl," Sarah continued, "is not like any other girl. She's smart, cunning and ambitious and is out for money. Didn't you see what happened the other night? There were so many beautiful and professional women at the party and who did Ken Campbell sit with all night? She was the only person he danced with. Don't tell me that girl is stupid or innocent. She knows that Ken Campbell has money."

"Sarah, leave the poor girl alone," I said.

It had crossed my mind, the idea of leaving Arshana in the house while I was away, but I chose not to think about it. I suppose my motives were selfish. For the past few weeks I had gotten quite accustomed to her, and I did not want to find her gone when I returned from my holidays. But speaking with Sarah had given me some food for thought. I felt slightly uneasy so I decided that I wanted to sit down with Arshana and have a long talk with her.

I knew she was in the garden with René so I decided to call her up and have my little talk with her, but when I looked through the window I saw that she was busy raking leaves and pilling them high under one of the huge oak trees.

Gladys, my Polish cleaning lady who came once a week to do the heavy cleaning, was fighting with René as usual. I couldn't remember a day since employing them when they were not at each other's throat.

"Why has the good Lord forgotten me?" I heard René saying. "He allowed that angel Betty to go, and has left you behind to torment me."

I too missed Betty, and was grateful to Arshana for filling the hole Betty left in my life. I hid behind the window and I could still hear René and Gladys fighting.

"How is your back, Gladys? Still on compensation?" René's voice was heavy with sarcasm.

"It is none of your damn business, René, and I'm going to let you in on my little secret: I am on permanent disability. I will never be able to do much hard work again. The only person I want to continue to work for is Mrs. Weissman. She's not a slave driver like the rest of them and she pays me very well. I am now going upstairs to have a word with her."

"When I last saw Mrs. Weissman, she had a headache," René said. "I guess she is probably resting now. And by the way Gladys, you shouldn't climb the stairs. You could hurt, your back."

Gladys hurled new obscenities at him, and to Arshana she said, "Would you please tell Mrs. Weissman that I will be coming over to-morrow morning to discuss something in private?"

"I will give Mrs. Weissman your message," Arshana said.

After Gladys left I pushed my head through the window and said, "Why don't you leave the raking until tomorrow, come on up and let us have some tea."

"Give us another 10 minutes more," Arshana said.

They spent another half hour and when they came into the kitchen, I said to René, "Why are you always on at Gladys? I believe you are secretly in love with her."

"Pardon me, Ma'am, but if she was the only woman on earth, I would die a saint. People like her know how to rip off this country. They are a burden to the honest taxpayers. They don't intend to work and make an honest living. There is absolutely nothing wrong with her, all she has to do is lose 100 pounds and all her aches and pain would disappear."

"René, let her be," Arshana said. "Let's have some tea and cookies."

I heard a car at the front gate and when I looked through the window, I saw David on the front step.

He came in and addressed Arshana, "You need a hat in the sun, don't expose your face to the sun. You don't want wrinkles, do you?"

"May I have a quick word with you, sir?" René asked David.

"What is it René? I'm in a terrible rush."

"Miss Arshana and I just made a $50 bet and I would like you to hold the stakes for safekeeping. You see, sir, without permission she pruned my rosebush and told me that by Christmas, the bush would be laden with roses and it would keep growing until it passed Mrs. Weissman's window.

"I told her that it would be very cold by then and there would be plenty of snow on the ground, but she said to me, 'René, put your money where your mouth is.'"

"Okay," David said. "Put your money on the kitchen table, I will collect it when I get home tonight."

"Mom," he said, as he walked into the kitchen. "I am in a rush, I just came home to pick up some papers. I am off to the Harbour Castle now to attend a meeting on behalf of Dr. Taylor. His plane was delayed in Calcutta. He was supposed to give a lecture on the eradication of leprosy. He's the main speaker so he asked me to go and explain his absence to the other speakers."

"Want something to eat?"

"No time, Mom, there is always plenty of food there," David said, running out the door.

I was still in the kitchen when Arshana came upstairs.

"Sit down Arshana, I must talk to you. As you know, I will be gone for three weeks and I don't think that I should leave you here when I'm gone."

"But why not, Mom? Where will I go? At the moment it is impossible for me to go over and stay at Sita's place. Yesterday when I was over there visiting, several boys and girls arrived from New York. They came with their suitcases. The suitcases were filled with drugs. The next day after I had arrived in Canada, a couple of cars came in from New York, and all day long people came in and out buying drugs. I was so scared of some of those people. I never want to be around them again."

"Arshana, I told everyone you had returned to Eleanor's, so what would I say if someone was to come and see you here?"

"No one will ever know I am here. I will stay in the house, lock the doors and never answer the phone. The only person who will know I am here is René and he will never tell anyone. I can even stay in his room. I will stay there when David has visitors. Gladys will be here tomorrow. Tell her that you will be away for three weeks, and that she can stay away until you return. In the meantime, I will do her job. It is also possible that I might get a flight back home. I had been to the travel agency a few times. In fact, the lady said that she had a cancellation last week, but she did not have a phone number to get in touch with me. She never gives out her phone number and I will never give yours out either. Please don't send me away."

I couldn't bear the thought of going on a holiday.

7

I thought things over all night. I closed my eyes with the hope that sleep would overtake me, but it didn't. My head was too full of frightening thoughts to induce sleep. I twisted and turned all night long and must have fallen asleep during the wee hours of the morning.

I heard talking in the kitchen and I slowly walked down the stairs and into the kitchen where I found René and Arshana having coffee. "Are you alright, Mom?" Arshana asked, pouring me a cup of coffee.

"I slept badly, Arshana. I kept going over and over in my mind whether I had made the right decision. I am prepared to let you stay here but I want you and René to promise me that no one will ever find out."

René said, "Ma'am, trust me, no one will walk through or drive through that gate unless I allow them to do so. Even if Dr. David wants to come in and come out, and I am not around, he will have to use his keys to open the gate. Ma'am please go and enjoy your holidays. All I ask of you is one favour: call Gladys and ask her not to come around here until you return."

I nodded. "Alright, René. And that reminds me, I have not had the opportunity to speak to David as yet concerning my decision. I was hoping to speak to him last night but he got home very late and I had already gone to bed."

"Ma'am, not to worry," René continued. "Dr. David always agrees with your decisions."

"It isn't David I am concerned about. It is Sarah and Martha. Hell will break loose if they were to find out that Arshana had not gone to Eleanor's."

"Oh, Dr. David is home already," René said, "Is he taking you to the airport?"

I was as confused as René. David came in and I asked, "Finished your meeting, David?"

"I cut it short so I could take you to the airport."

"I thought Cynthia was driving us," I said.

"Yes, she was supposed to," David said. "But since I am home early I will drive. It is better that I do the driving anyways, because there is always construction going on around the airport and if you miss a sign you are in hell. You will have to drive around and around. The last time I was at the airport, even the taxi driver who took us got lost."

"David, I didn't have the chance to speak to you last night but as you are aware, I am leaving Arshana in the house. I didn't want anyone to know, especially Martha and Sarah. You know what they would think."

"Who cares what they think? Mom, I have told you time and again to start living your life the way you want to. Ignore what other people think."

"It's not that easy, David. Anyways there is plenty of food in the freezer and René will be around if Arshana needs anything. She is not to leave the house. She knows that."

The phone rang. David answered it. It was Cynthia. I heard him say to her, "Cynthia, stop being childish. Why don't you grow up? I said I am driving, and that means I am driving."

When he hung up, I said to him, "David, why don't you marry Cynthia. She loves you."

"Cynthia does not love me, Mom. Cynthia loves the idea of being married to Dr. Weissman. She loves black tie affairs, elaborate dinner parties and an extravagant social life. I don't. After a hard day's work at the office, I want to come home and relax. I don't want to go to clubs or bars or to eat out. I want to find a nice home cooked dinner waiting for me. I don't mind going to the occasional party but I am not a party person. You yourself have told me umpteen times that whenever I go to a party, I stand in a corner like a statue. Right now, I am just looking forward to going to India with Dr. Taylor. He is trying to get me more involved with his work in Indrapur."

"David, David," I said "Cynthia is here. I don't want her coming upstairs. Let's go."

I quickly kissed Arshana goodbye. As I did so, I saw tears streaming down her cheeks.

"You told me," she said, "that there is a strong possibility that you might go to Guyana. If you do, please visit my grandmother."

"As you know, Arshana, I am travelling with three other ladies, but if I find it at all possible, I will surely visit your grandmother. Now you take care of yourself until I return."

"Time to go, Mom," David said. "Can you hear that nut blowing her horn?" David picked up my suitcase and went to put it in his trunk.

"We're taking my car," Cynthia said. "You have no right to change my plans."

"Cynthia, give me your keys. I'd like to put your mother's suitcase into my trunk. And you be a good girl and hop into my car."

Reluctantly she handed him the keys.

"All aboard," David said, "and fasten your seatbelts. We don't want to be stopped by police."

"They will charge you, not me," Cynthia said.

"Auntie Martha, where did you get this stubborn, miserable daughter from?"

"She certainly didn't get her stubbornness from me," Martha replied. "She must have gotten it from her father."

There was little traffic so it took us less than twenty minutes to get to the airport.

Sarah, Joanne and Ramona were already there and had arranged for a porter to collect our bags.

"Don't get out of the car," I said to both Cynthia and David. "The policeman is waving drivers on."

However, David quickly got out of the car, took our bags from the trunk, kissed us quickly and drove away.

The porter took our bags to the British West Indies first-class counter. There was no lineup so it took us no time to get our tickets and then we headed for security. There was a bit of hold up there, but after we were through we went straight into the first class lounge. We waited for more than an hour and when boarding began, we and the other first-class passengers were told to board first.

As we were boarding the plane, a young woman with a baby in her arms turned to me and said we were lucky. The British West Indies Airline planes rarely left on time.

When we got in the plane, we took our seats and waited for the other passengers to board. We were all seated and about to buckle up when we heard an announcement from the captain telling us to disembark. Angry passengers were cursing and children were screaming, but we had no choice but to disembark.

People with kids tried to get to the restaurants to get their children something to eat, but there were long lines and not enough seats in the restaurant or bars to accommodate all the people. Luckily, we were in first class, so we just returned to the lounge and relaxed.

Two hours later we were told to board the plane once again and we took off just before midnight.

We arrived in the Port of Spain in Trinidad at 6 o'clock the next morning, and by 8 o'clock we were finally at our hotel.

It was already beginning to get hot. After we checked into the rooms, Sarah and Joanne, not wanting to miss any sun, quickly changed into their bathing suits and headed for the pool. Since we had very little sleep the night before, Martha and I decided to sleep until lunchtime. Just before lunch, Joanne came up and told us that a seafood buffet was being set up next to the swimming pool.

Martha was still half asleep, but called out that a buffet sounded good. "I'm famished," she said. "Why don't you go ahead and start things up, I'll be down in two seconds."

The buffet was scrumptious. Every type of seafood was laid out on the table. The place was packed. There was one table left and that was a table for eight. We were lucky to get that table. As we were eating, two American couples came in and asked if they could join us.

"Do we have a choice?" Sarah asked jokingly.

As we were eating, one of the ladies asked whether we were enjoying Trinidad.

"We arrived from Canada only this morning," Martha said. "So we haven't had a chance to see or do anything yet."

The American lady said "after lunch we're doing a tour of the city. I think that there are still seats left on the bus. Would you folks care to join?"

Without even asking us, Joanne said, "why not?"

The city tour was not very interesting. The only thing of interest we saw as we drove around the harbour was a cruise ship leaving the port. "Why don't we leave the bus?" one of the American men said, "We can walk around by ourselves for a while, then we can find a bar and go in and have a nice drink."

"Splendid idea," Joanne said. "Tom, is that your name?" She addressed the man who had suggested the bar, saying, "you actually read my mind."

To be social, I tried to enjoy a drink with the others, until I noticed a travel agency just across the street.

"If you folks don't mind, I'd like to slip over to that travel agency. I'd like to pick up a few brochures," I said.

"That'll give us time for another drink," Joanne said.

Traffic was heavy and the nearest crosswalk was several blocks away, but I did manage to go to the travel agency and collect some brochures.

Laura, one of the American women, said to me, "I see you have picked up some brochures on Guyana. We just visited there. The people are fantastic, but you have to be very careful. It is advisable not to go out at night, but if you do so, never walk with a purse. A must-see is the Kaieteur Falls, but if you don't like helicopters, the ship could be very bumpy."

"We have plenty of time to decide," Martha said. "We're thinking of Guyana or Venezuela."

"We better head back to the hotel now," Tom said. "We have to take two cabs. And if you girls care to join us, we are having dinner at 7 o'clock."

"That would be nice," Sarah said. "But first we're going to our rooms and looking through the brochures."

As we were looking through the brochures, Martha said to me, "Ruth, isn't Guyana the place where what's-her-name is from?"

"What are you talking about?" I asked.

"Ruth, you know damn well who I'm talking about. Don't be dumb with me."

"If you are referring to Arshana, yes, she is from Guyana."

Joanne said, "I don't think there's too much to see in Georgetown, but from the pictures I'm looking at in the brochure, it seems that there's plenty to see in the interior. Apparently, lots of plane trips are available every day. We could always go on one of the day trips. I heard that there are lots of shops where you can buy gold and diamond jewelry. Sindhu, one of Jenny's friends, always wears tons of jewelry. You should see her bracelets. She bought them all from Guyana."

"How far is it from here to Guyana?" Sarah asked.

"Only about one to two hours," I said.

"Ruth, do you want to go there?" Martha asked.

"I'm easy. Wherever you all decide to go, I'll go." I didn't want to show any enthusiasm.

"Well, I am happy to go to Guyana," Joanne said.

"You are happy to go there because you heard of all the gold and diamonds there," Sarah said.

"So to Guyana we will go," laughed Martha. "And don't forget we're still supposed to meet those folks for dinner."

We got dressed and went down to the restaurant. The Americans were already there. They were sitting in the garden on beautiful wicker furniture, sipping piña coladas. Several orchid vines laden with purple flowers added charm to the well-kept garden. Beautiful parrots and colourful macaws flew from branch to branch on the nearby trees and then all of a sudden one of the parrots landed on our table.

"Don't encourage him, Stanley," the American woman said to her husband.

"He only wants a plantain chip, Dorothy," Stanley responded.

"Get him off the table, Stanley. Right now! Yesterday he almost bit me."

"No, he didn't. He's a tame bird. He wouldn't bite anyone."

"Put your fingers in his mouth. You'll find out."

"Dorothy is always miserable when she's hungry," Stanley said. "Are you folks ready to eat? You can stay for another drink if you'd like."

"I'm quite hungry," Martha said.

"Me too," Joanne said.

"Then off to dinner we go," said Stanley.

Being a garden lover, I would have liked to remain a little longer in the garden to check out some of the tropical plants, but I had no choice but to follow the group into dinner.

The dinner was superb. We thanked the waiter for the dinner selections he had suggested, and then we went for a coffee in the lounge where we could drink it comfortably. After coffee and liqueur, the

Americans excused themselves, and we exchanged addresses, telephone numbers and kisses before they left.

Our time in Trinidad was great. During the day, if we did not use our hotel pool, we would go to the beach and bargain with the vendors. At night, after dinner we would sit in the lounge, drink coffee and liqueur and listen to the calypso band. Most of the time Joanne would start the party. Sarah had said Joanne would be fun to travel with, and she was right. Joanne would hop onto the dancefloor, shout 'party time' and the band would begin to play. Everyone, whether they had partners or not would get on the floor and dance to the music.

8

We enjoyed all our days and fun-filled nights in Trinidad, but on the 17th day of our vacation we boarded a small plane for Guyana.

The plane was full, but except for one other passenger, we were the only ones in first class. As soon as we were all settled and the plane was in the air, the stewardess came around with champagne.

The young man, who was the other first-class passenger, lifted his glass and said, "Cheers!"

"Where are you ladies from?" he asked.

"Canada," we all replied simultaneously. "I'm from Canada too. I'm employed in the Canadian embassy in Guyana. If it isn't too presumptuous of me, may I ask why you ladies are going to Guyana?"

We struck up an easy conversation.

"Pardon me," he said jokingly, "it's just that from the way you ladies have already finished one bottle of champagne, I'm guessing that you aren't missionaries."

"We've heard about Guyana and since we were in Trinidad, and Guyana isn't so far away, we decided to visit and see what it's like," Martha said.

"You girls know anyone there?"

"Not a soul," Joanne replied. "When we were in Trinidad, we were looking through some brochures and we read about the Orinoco River, the Pacaraima Mountains and the Kaieteur Falls, so we decided to visit."

"Which one of the hotels are you folks staying at?"

"We haven't booked the hotel," Joanne said.

"By the way, my name is Stephen and I have to give it to you, you are very adventurous. When we land at the Cheddi Jagan airport, I will make a few phone calls. There is a nice hotel not too far from the embassy and I'll try and see if I can get you ladies a couple of rooms there. I know the guy who runs the hotel."

After we landed, Stephen, being a diplomat, had no problem with the customs and since all of us had carry-on bags, he helped us to get through customs in no time. A chauffeur was waiting for Stephen who offered us a ride into town. He said it would be a bit of a squeeze but he would feel better if he got us safely in a hotel. As we were drawing into Georgetown, Stephen tried to phone the hotel several times but couldn't get through. As we got closer to the city, he was able to reach the hotel and told us that he was able to get us two rooms. On arriving at the hotel, he accompanied us to the reception desk. When we were registered, he said goodbye with a final warning not to leave the hotel at night.

The rooms were comfortable enough, with an open door between the two rooms. We relaxed a little while, then decided that we should go and check out the hotel bar and have a few drinks before dinner. Martha and Joanne sat at the bar and chatted with the bartender. Sarah and I choose to sit in the lounge on the comfortable bamboo chairs and try the local wine.

When the waiter brought us the wine, he told us that if we were planning to eat, we should go into the dining room right away. "Thank you, I said to the waiter. Now get us a nice table and tell the other two ladies at the bar to meet us in the dining room."

He found a nice table, and after we were seated, handed us each a menu. As I looked through the menu, I said, "I know what I'm going to order. I want the stewed snapper and fried plantains."

"Have you had that before, Ruth?" Sarah asked.

"Arshana made it several times. In fact, John ate it once at my place and loved it. In fact, every time he sees Arshana, he asks her when she will make some more stewed fish for him."

"That pig eats anything that isn't marked down," Sarah said.

"Don't be mean, Sarah. Try the fish, you might like it too," I said.

When the waiter returned to take our order, Joanne said to him,

"My friend here has suggested the snapper. What do you think?"

"It is the best choice on the menu. You will all enjoy it."

Everyone decided on the snapper and we all enjoyed it.

"Coffee and liqueur for anyone?" the waiter asked.

"Certainly," Joanne said.

"And may I make two suggestions to you ladies?" the waiter continued. "One: try the cherry liqueur and two: go and secure your seat in the lounge right away. I'll serve you coffee and liqueur there. Tonight is steel band night and the place will be packed like sardines."

The waiter was right. The lounge was already crowded, but he was able to get us a comfortable table a little distant from the band. "If you sit any closer to the band, you will be deaf by the time you leave here tonight."

We had barely sat down when we saw Stephen walking towards our table.

"I had every intention of asking you ladies to dinner tonight, but I fell asleep and I just got up," he said.

"We had a lovely dinner," Sarah told him. "You sit down, if you can find a chair, and we will buy you a drink."

"Hi, Mr. Stephen," the waiter said as he returned with our coffee and liqueur. "Will you be having your usual, sir?" the waiter asked.

"Yes Sam, my usual rum and coconut water."

"Did you say rum and coconut water?" Joanne asked.

"Yes Ma'am," Stephen said.

"Well, that is a first for me. I thought I had tried every possible combination of drinks under the sun, but I have never heard of that combination."

"Try one later, you might like it," he said to Joanne.

Then he said to us, "Did I hear one of you ladies mention something about the Kaieteur Falls? If you are interested, there is Charles over there. He takes tours to the falls."

"Oh, we would like to see the falls," Martha said.

"I'll call Charles," Stephen said, then turned to look for someone behind our table. "Hi Charles," he called out, "come over here for a minute."

A bulky man came walking towards our table. Introducing us to Charles, Stephen said, "These ladies would like to visit the falls."

"I'm taking a couple from England tomorrow morning but I do

have space for the four ladies."

"Charles?" I said, "I understand that only helicopters go to the falls. Is that true?"

"Yes, only helicopters go to the falls. They can maneuver easily around the falls."

"You can count me out, Charles," I said. "I will not be flying in a helicopter."

Charles left and said that he was off to make necessary arrangements for the trip the next morning.

The lounge was beginning to get more crowded. Some people were actually standing around, so after our coffee and liqueur, we tried the rum and coconut water, said goodnight to Stephen and went to our rooms.

9

Heavy window shades did nothing to prevent the hot tropical sun from filtering into our room, so I, not wanting to disturb Martha, got out of bed and opened one of our windows quietly. A rush of perfume came swirling into the room. I was certain that the sweet scent came from the jasmine vine and the morning glory bush that was in full bloom beneath our window. I inhaled and exhaled a few times, breathing in that soothing fresh air. It was beginning to get hot, although it had rained all night.

"Ruth, are you up already?" I heard Martha's voice calling out to me, "I am tired. I want to sleep some more."

"I bet Joanne is tired also," I said. "We came up to our rooms at a reasonable hour, so why did you and Joanne return to the bar? You should've gone to bed."

"We weren't feeling tired so we went down to the bar for a night cap. And please remember, Ruth, I am on vacation."

Sarah heard us talking and she called out from the room, "What time is it?"

"Time to get up, if you don't want to miss your tour. We should have been down to breakfast half an hour ago."

We quickly got showered and dressed and went down to the dining room.

As soon as we were seated, the waiter brought us mango juice and coffee. He then pointed out a table to us. The table was filled with an assortment of breads. Lots of roll sweetbreads, coconut bread and coconut-filled donuts. The table next to it had a variety of tropical fruits, papayas, mangoes, pineapple, sour sap and other fruits which we were not familiar with.

Over breakfast, Martha begged me to change my mind and accompany them on the trip, but I stuck to my guns.

"No helicopters for me."

As we were about to finish our breakfast, we saw Charles walking towards our table.

"Good morning, ladies," he said, bowing. I hope you had a good night's sleep. Don't rush, we have some time. Finish your breakfast and meet me in the lounge afterwards."

The English couple was already there and they sat sipping coffee with Charles. He introduced the couple to us, and as he did so, he said, "I have some unpleasant news for you. There was an unexpected death in my family and I will be unable to accompany you on the tour. I tried to find a replacement, but couldn't find anyone at such short notice. However, the tour is still available and the pilot is willing to fly you there. If you all are still willing to take the tour, I can sit down and explain everything you will see. It is exactly what I would've said to you if I were on the tour."

The English couple were returning to England that very night and since we had just one more day, the girls decided to take the tour. As Joanne had said to Charles, our main interest was to see the falls.

"Trust me," Charles said, "seeing the falls is an unforgettable experience. You won't regret it. And now I'll tell you a little about what you will see."

Since I was not doing the tour, I decided to sit and listen to what Charles had to say. Most of the time they would be flying over dense forest, a sanctuary for wild animals and exotic birds. These creatures lived peacefully, without any human interference in their natural habitat. They would see several smaller falls on the way, but that would be nothing in comparison to the majestic Kaieteur Falls. According to Charles, though many people had never heard of the Kaieteur Falls, it was one of the highest falls in the world! The drop is five times higher than Niagara Falls.

"You are all so lucky," Charles continued. "It is a beautiful morning and the morning tours are usually the best ones to take. You should arrive there around 11 o'clock. Just before reaching the falls, the pilot will make an announcement. Then he will circle the falls for about 10 minutes, enabling everyone to get a good view. On your way back, when all the excitement of seeing the falls is over, I usually give a talk about the history of Guyana. Of course, I always tell the folks that will cost extra," he said jokingly.

"I am always surprised by how little people know about Guyana. I was shocked last week when a passenger on the plane said to me that he thought Guyana and Ghana were the same place! Did you know that Guyana is the only English-speaking country in South America? It was discovered by Christopher Columbus and he lost interest in it shortly after, but Sir Walter Raleigh saw potential for a settlement. The Dutch saw even more potential, and they settled here, but after numerous trysts, the British took over and named the country British Guyana. They wanted to make sure that it was separated from the other Guyanas. The Dutch Guyana and the French Guyana.

"Guyana is now independent, but because of its instability, half of its people are living in other countries all over the world."

Charles stopped suddenly and said, "Sorry folks, no more information. I can see your bus driver coming to take you to your plane so I am going to say goodbye for now and hope that you enjoy your tour."

I was glad that I had the opportunity to listen to Charles's information on Guyana. As soon as the girls left, I headed straight to the information desk. A beautiful brown-skinned woman was sitting at the desk. Her hands jangled with gold bracelets, and she wore long dangling earrings. Her name tag read 'Doreen.' She smiled as I approached her, and I couldn't help but notice her perfectly white teeth.

"I noticed that you did not go with your friends. Is there anything I can do for you?" Doreen asked.

"I would like you to recommend a good taxi driver for me. Someone to drive me around a bit."

"Any place in particular you would like to go?"

"I heard of a place called Kitty and if it isn't too far from here I would like to go there."

"Kitty," she said, "that isn't very far. I know the best person to take you there. He lives in Kitty. I don't know what happened to him today. I'm surprised he isn't here yet... Oh my God, speak of the devil, there he is."

She called out to the man who had just come in, "Ram, Ram! Come here."

Ram came walking towards us smiling and flashing two permanent gold teeth. "Ram, I hope you haven't got any customers yet because I have a job for you. I want you to take this nice lady to Kitty."

"No problem, I am free."

And to me, he asked, "Would you like to go now or later? Later might be too hot for you."

"I can go now if you are ready," I said.

"Oh I am quite ready, Ma'am, let's go."

As we were leaving, Doreen said to Ram, "Hi, when you come back, I want my small juice."

"You know I always fix you up," Ram said as he led me through the hotel and down to the taxi. "Where about in Kitty would you like to go?" Ram asked me.

"Pike street?"

"Pike Street!" Ram said. "I live on Pike Street. I know everyone there."

"I have an address here for a Mrs. Lilly Persaud."

"You mean Auntie Lilly! I live just two doors away from her." He looked surprised and excited. "Auntie Lilly is a dear old lady. Everyone on the street loves her. All day long she sits by her window and calls out to everyone as they pass by."

As we turned into Pike Street, Ram stopped the taxi and said "You see that little park there? One of our prime ministers lives there. I didn't know if you've ever heard of him. His name was Forbes Burnham."

"I really don't know too much about Guyana, Ram."

Pointing out Auntie Lilly's house out to me, Ram said, "Remember what I told you. She is sitting at her window."

Ram opened the taxi door for me and when I got out, he called towards the house saying, "I got a visitor from Canada to see you, Auntie."

"Is that you, Ram?" Auntie Lilly asked. "If you brought a visitor to see me, why don't you bring her up? I'll call Tulsi to open the front door."

When I reached the top of the stairs, a young woman with two long braids opened the door for me. As soon as I entered the house, the first thing I noticed was that the place was spotless. Auntie Lilly herself was a dignified looking old lady. She was sitting on a rocking chair, dressed in a beautiful pink housecoat with matching fluffy slippers. Perched on the back of her chair was a macaw who kept walking from side to side.

"Be still, Peter," she said to the macaw. "Behave yourself, we have a visitor. She is from Canada. Remember I told you that Arshana is in Canada."

"Arshana, Arshana," the macaw said.

"Peter and I say a prayer for Arshana every morning," Auntie Lilly said. "Don't we, Peter?"

"Arshana, Arshana," Peter kept saying.

"Peter, I'd like to talk to this nice lady. One more sound from you and I will put you in your cage, do you hear me?"

I never heard another sound from Peter again.

"So you are from Canada," she said to me. "You have come to see me because you have met my Arshana. I hope you have brought me some good news about her. I know it takes a long time to get letters from Canada, but since she left I have only received two letters from her and I'm so worried."

Ram guided me up the stairs and was standing next to my chair.

"Why don't you sit down, Ram?" Auntie Lilly said.

"Thank you, Auntie," Ram said. "I have to run home for a while and I will leave you two to chat. I will return in a little while." Then to me he said, "Ma'am, if you want to leave before I return, send Tulsi to call me."

Then Auntie Lilly said, "Madam, please tell me how my Arshana is doing. Is she working? Has she found a good job? I sent her some money last week. Another girl from the bank was going to join them, so she took the money for me.

"I miss my Arshana so much. She is a decent girl. I brought her up to be honest and respectful. She went to a private school run by nuns and then I sent her to a cooking school. When she was here, people always asked her to cook for their parties. You should ask her to cook for you sometimes. She's a good cook."

Auntie stopped talking for a moment and she bent her head. There were tears in her eyes. "I wonder sometimes if I did the right thing by allowing her to go to Canada, but every day things get worse in this country and I wanted a better life for her. You know I paid for her to get a visa to go to Canada? She had a good job at the bank. The manager came to see me last week. I think he liked my Arshana also. He said her job would be waiting for her anytime she returned. I hope Sita and Rita found her a good job as they promised.

"Oh, forgive me, Ma'am, I am here babbling away and I have not offered you anything to eat or drink. Where are my manners?"

"Tulsi, Tulsi," she called out. The young woman appeared.

"Yes Auntie?" she said.

"Bring Ma'am a tall glass of sorrel drink. Fill it up with ice and get a piece of cassava pone for her."

"Yes Auntie."

Tulsi left and Auntie Lilly said to me, "There isn't a day that goes by that I do not sit and cry for my Arshana. I keep on asking myself if I did the right thing by allowing her to go to Canada. But Sita and Rita kept writing and phoning and eventually I gave in and she promised that if things didn't work out, she would return home immediately. You wouldn't believe how many young men from well-to-do families wanted to marry her but she found something wrong with each and every one of them. She was so hard to please.

"I forgot to ask you whether you met Vishnu," said Auntie Lilly.

"No, I didn't" I said.

"He was here in August and he brought along one of his friends from medical school for a little holiday. They enjoyed themselves when they were here. Every morning they came over here and had breakfast with me. Tulsi cooked all sorts of dishes for them. The young man, Vishnu's friend, enjoyed Guyanese food. I told him that Arshana is a really good cook and he and Vishnu should try to find her when they return to Canada. They go to school in Montréal and they told me that Montréal is far from Toronto, but the next time they visit Toronto they are certainly going to look her up. Vishnu's brother is a doctor and he takes good care of me. He wanted to marry my Arshana also, but he is a little bald," she cackled. "Arshana is so full of humor. You know what she said to him? 'Grow some hair on your head and I will marry you.'"

Auntie Lilly kept talking and I enjoyed listening to her. She was so happy to talk about Arshana. "Have you seen Arshana's pictures on the wall?" she asked me. "You can't see the pictures properly from where you're sitting. Turn your chair around."

I did as she directed. There was a whole wall dedicated to Arshana.

Pictures from when she was a baby, pictures when she was a teenager and a more recent photo that took up a good part of the wall.

"In one of her letters, Arshana mentioned that she had met a very kind lady. Are you by any chance that lady?"

I was glad that I did not have to answer her, because just then Tulsi arrived with the drink and the cassava pone.

It was a hot day and the drink was very refreshing. I nearly drank it all at once. And when I was offered a second glass, I accepted. As I sat and listened to her talk, I kept wondering whether or not I should offer some money. She didn't look as though she was in need of anything. I kept weighing the decision in my mind, and then suddenly she put her hand in her bosom and pulled out a little cloth purse. The purse was held together by a long string. She opened the purse and slowly counted out 500 Canadian and 500 American dollars and handed it to me.

"Give this money to Arshana for me. I think I can trust you. At my age, I have to be careful whom I trust."

"I rent a couple of rooms downstairs. With the rent money I exchange American dollars from Mrs. Alsop and Canadian dollars from Mrs. Maray. They have children living abroad and every time they receive money from them they would come over and change it with me. Ram also gives me all of the foreign money he collects. I give them all a better rate than the bank," she laughed. "Maybe I am 92. But I have all my senses. I can hear, I don't wear glasses and I have quite a few of my own teeth."

She needed little encouragement to continue her one-sided conversation.

"I'm a bit of a psychic," she continued. "How do you think I knew there was a woman from Canada at my door? I can see into the future. Right now my Arshana is going through a very hard period in her life. It will last for quite a while but I'm not concerned because I can see a future for her at the end of the rainbow. Her future is not silver or gold, but a future of diamonds. She will eventually be happy. My time on earth is limited. I know that I will never see my Arshana again, but when I am in heaven close to my Maker, I will make damn sure that my Arshana is comfortable on earth.

"I believe Ram is coming to get you," she said. "He is teasing Sadhoo as usual." When I looked through the window, I saw a skinny man who reminded me so much of Mahatma Gandhi. He carried a long stick and all he wore was a loincloth.

Ram came running up the stairs and I heard him say to the Gandhi-lookalike, "Can I borrow $1000 from you?"

"Ram, why don't you behave yourself?" Auntie Lilly said, "Leave the poor Sadhoo."

"Poor Sadhoo," Ram scoffed as he walked through the door. "Sadhoo has more money hidden under his mattress than you could ever dream off."

"Now Ram, you go into the kitchen and tell Tulsi to give him something to eat." Ram went to the kitchen and returned with two very ripe mangoes.

"Just picked them off my tree," he said. "You can eat them when you return to the hotel."

"Thank you, Ram," I said. "But I think we ought to return to the hotel now and let Auntie Lilly have some rest. I've already taken up plenty of her time."

"I have all the time in the world," she said. She then got up, threw her arms around me and kissed me. Her eyes were now filled with tears.

"Please kiss my Arshana for me; I know I'll never have the opportunity to kiss her ever again." My eyes became teary too. I kissed her, said goodbye and walked slowly down the stairs.

As we drove away, Ram said to me, "She is waving goodbye. Isn't she a dear old lady? Tell Arshana not to worry about her. We all love her. All the neighbours do. We live like family. I don't know if you noticed, but I just walked into her kitchen and had something to eat.

"The people in the house next door are very kind to her. One son is a doctor and the other is a judge. That judge is her executer. If anything should happen to her before Arshana returns, he would definitely see to everything."

As we waved goodbye, Ram said, "Care to do a bit of sight-seeing before we return to the hotel?"

"No, Ram. The heat is beginning to give me a headache. I would like to return to the hotel. I hope they have fixed the air conditioning. They tried to fix it last night, but it made so much noise afterwards that we had to turn it off so we could get some sleep."

On our way back to the hotel, Ram drove along the east coast and I was able to feel the nice cool breeze blowing in from the Atlantic. When we reached the hotel, he said to me, "Now you hold on to your purse. As a matter of fact," he continued, "I'll walk you into the hotel. I don't like the look of some of these scary characters hanging around. The hotel tries to keep them away by calling the police, but there's very little the police are able to do. They go away for a couple of hours and then return."

"Ram, are you going to be around the hotel later this evening?" I asked him.

"If you would like me to Ma'am, I could hang around."

"I don't believe my friends will be back yet from their visit to the falls. However as soon as they get here, I'll see what our plans are for tomorrow and I'll let you know."

"I'd appreciate that very much, Ma'am."

I went straight to my room, changed my clothes and got into my dressing gown. Then I got into bed with every intention of falling asleep, but the noise from the air conditioner made it impossible. I closed my eyes and thought of that dear lady Auntie Lilly. She loved her grand-daughter and I was glad that Arshana had not let her know what she was going through. I sincerely believed that, had I not taken Arshana into my house, she would have returned to Guyana and enjoyed her life under the watchful and protective eye of her grandmother. I promised myself that as soon as I returned to Canada, I was going to encourage Arshana to return home. With such positive thoughts in my mind, I closed my eyes.

10

I must've dozed off because I was not even aware that Martha had entered the room till she spoke up.

"Ruth, are you asleep?" She asked.

"Not anymore."

Sarah and Joanne heard us talking and came over to my room.

Sarah threw herself on my bed and said, "Never ever again am I going on a helicopter. I threw up all the way there and all the way back."

"You two don't look too good either," I said to Martha and Joanne.

"Ruth, you are always the smart one," Sarah said. "I should have listened to you and never gone on that trip."

"Order some tea now, and later we can have dinner in our room," I said.

"Splendid idea," Joanne said. "That plane ride, although I was glad I went on it, has sapped all the energy out of me. I don't feel like dressing up for dinner."

We ordered dinner in our room, chatted for a while and then decided to make it an early night. We found it difficult to sleep. The noise from the air conditioner was unbearable, so we turned it off.

I could hear Joanne in the other room telling Sarah, "Let's open the windows."

From my room I shouted, "Don't. If you do, it will create another problem. One of the maids told me never to open the windows at night;

'mosquitoes would eat you alive,' she said."

We all tried to sleep but none of us had a good night's rest. We were all up by daybreak.

"Put on the least clothes as possible," Sarah shouted from her room. "It's going to be a very hot day."

After we were dressed, we went down for breakfast. I saw Ram as we were about to go into the dining room. He was standing at the reception desk talking with Doreen.

"Did you have a good night's sleep?" he asked as he came walking towards me.

"I can't say I did, Ram."

"Do you know this guy, Ruth?" Martha asked.

"I met him yesterday. He took me where I wanted to go. If you plan to do any shopping or sightseeing I would strongly recommend him."

"If he has a taxi," Joanne said, "I'll go with him, but neither Sarah nor I would go again in one of the helicopters."

"Ram, why don't you wait around here?" I said. "Let's eat first, and over breakfast we'll decide what we want to do."

"Take your time. Enjoy your breakfast. I will be waiting just by the reception desk."

Over breakfast it was decided that we would drive around a little, see what we could of the city and then go shopping.

Ram was waiting for us at the reception desk when we came out of the dining room, and when we told him what we had decided, he took us to his taxi.

"To be honest," Ram said, "there isn't much to see in the city, but I'll drive you around a little. On the way I will point out some of the government buildings and then I will take you across the Demerara River."

There wasn't much to see, as Ram had said, so he drove us across a long bridge before we reached the other side of the river. Then Ram stopped the taxi in front of a cart laden with water coconuts.

"How are we doing today?" the vendor said to Ram. "And what can I do for you?"

"You can dive down to the bottom of the cart and bring up some fresh coconuts for me. And I don't want you pulling any of your tricks on me."

"What are you saying, Ram? I'm always nice to beautiful ladies."

"No sweet talk, Henry. Start cutting the coconuts."

Henry took a cutlass knife and lopped the top off each of the coconuts and gave us one each.

"Wait, I'll give you all a straw. I don't want you to spoil your pretty dresses."

After we had finished with the water, Henry split the coconuts in half and we ate the jelly. "Want more?" Ram asked.

"This coconut tastes so good," Martha said. "Had I known, I would have had coconuts for breakfast?"

"Sure you don't want more coconuts, ladies?" Ram asked. "If not, let's go." And without saying anything to us, he paid Henry for the coconuts. In the taxi, Ram told us that if we had tried to pay Henry, he would have charged us double the price. "Now, do you want to drive around on the side of the river or do you want to shop?"

"Shop!" Joanne said.

When we were back in the city, Ram pointed to a large covered building.

"That's the Starbroek Market. Anything you want, you can buy there. There are lots of jewelry shops, but I would rather you didn't go there. Too many crooks and pickpockets in the area and they can spot a tourist from miles away.

"If I may suggest, I could take you all to a very nice jewelry shop. Some people think I take them there because I get a commission but that's far from the truth. I take people there because the area is protected by guards and they wouldn't think twice to shoot if anyone tried to rob you. And another thing, whatever you buy there is genuine. If a piece of jewelry is stamped 18 karat gold, you can rest assured that you are getting 18 karat gold. I can't say that for the jewelry you would buy in the market. It might be cheaper but you are not getting what you paid for."

"Well take us there, now," Joanne said.

On our way to the jewelry shop, Ram stopped in front of a huge building.

He said, "That's the St. George Cathedral, the largest wooden building in the world."

"I read about it in one of the brochures," Sarah said, "I'm glad I saw it."

"At the moment they are doing some renovations, but if you folks would like to go inside, I could arrange it," Ram said.

"Let's go to the jewelry shop," Joanne said. "If anyone asks, we can say we saw it."

Ten minutes later we arrived at the jewelry shop. Ram told us to sit in the car and make sure that the windows were rolled up. He blew his horn and one of the guards who was standing in front of the shop came running towards the car. He was carrying a gun on his shoulders.

"These ladies have come to do some shopping," Ram said. "But I don't like the look of those two guys standing across the street."

"Don't worry," the guard said. "I've had my eyes on them all morning; trust me, if they try anything, I will blow their brains out."

He then gave a sign to another guard and they both escorted us into the shop. One guard pressed a button and the door was closed behind us.

There were no other customers in the shop, so all three of the saleswomen attended to us immediately. They took out several trays of jewelry from the showcases. Joanne, Sarah and Martha went wild. But I saw one of the overstuffed chairs and rested my legs.

"Aren't you buying anything?" Ram asked me.

"Those women have daughters, I only have one son. And my husband bought me so much jewelry when he was alive that I would never be able to wear them all in this lifetime. I hope I have plenty of granddaughters to give jewelry to. But Ram, I do like that chain and pendant you're wearing. I have seen it before and I can't remember where."

"I know where you saw it," Ram said. "You saw it at Auntie Lilly's house yesterday. There's a huge framed picture of Arshana on the wall, and she is wearing one of these Aums."

"Aum? What is an Aum?" I asked.

"Hindus wear it, the same way you would wear a cross or any other religious symbol. There's a whole tray filled with them. People, when they come from abroad, always buy them to take back home to friends and relatives."

"I'll take a nice one. Ram, choose one for me."

"It depends on how much you want to spend, Ma'am."

"Don't worry about the price."

Ram picked up a beautiful Aum that was encrusted with diamonds. "It is the most beautiful piece in the showcase and it is also the most expensive piece."

"I'll take it Ram. And it already has a chain on it."

"Wait a minute," Ram said. "Don't say a word."

He called one of the saleswomen over and, holding the chain and pendant in his hand, he said, "As you can see, this lady isn't buying too much, and she likes this piece but it is a little too expensive for her."

The saleswoman nodded. "This lady has good taste. That piece is one of a kind. You would never see that design anywhere else. We rarely make pieces like those. It costs us too much to make, so we have to sell it at a high price. But let me speak to my boss and see if she can reduce it a bit."

The boss was sitting in a glass office so the saleswoman didn't have to move to beckon her to come over. When she came over, she gave us the same sales pitch that we had just heard from the saleswoman. For a few seconds she turned the pendant around and around in her hand and asked me whether I was with the other ladies.

She had noticed the huge selection the girls had in front of them, and turning to the saleswoman, she said, "take 20% off." And to me she said, "You have a very unique piece. The person wearing it will definitely enjoy it."

After I paid for it and had it wrapped, Ram took it from me and put it in his pocket.

Martha, Sarah and Joanne had piles of jewelry in front of them.

"Don't pay what they ask," Ram said quietly to the girls, "ask for a cut."

"I see you, Ram," the saleswoman said. "Are you teaching these women how to shop?"

"I haven't said a word to them," Ram said.

"Okay Ram, I believe you. Anyway the boss agreed to take a further 10% off. And that is on top of the sale price."

"That's good of you," Ram said. "Just wrap up all the purchases and call up the guards to walk us out."

As we entered the taxi, Ram said, "I suggest we return to the hotel. It isn't safe to be walking around with all the jewelry you have bought." We all agreed and Ram took us back to the hotel.

We had planned to take the hotel shuttle to the airport, but since it was four of us, we decided that it would not only be more economical but more convenient for Ram to take us to the airport.

It was a scenic drive to the airport. Ram drove slowly, even stopping a couple of times to buy us some fresh fruit and cold drinks, yet we got to the airport with lots of time to spare.

We thanked Ram for being such a good friend, paid him and said goodbye.

As he was about to drive off, 1 waved to him to stop. He stopped the taxi and came walking towards me. I gave him an additional $100, my phone number and address and told him that if anything should happen to Auntie Lilly before Arshana returned, he should let me know immediately.

"You can count on me, Ma'am. I'll let you know."

"Ruth, why did you go back to talk to Ram?" Martha asked. They were waiting for me outside the airport and we all went in together.

"I wanted him to say a special thank you to Arshana's grandmother. He took me to visit her. I saw Arshana's home and where she came from and I promised myself that if anyone should say anything disrespectful to her, that person will get a tongue-lashing from me and I mean it."

"Is her family that rich?" Sarah asked.

"What they have, Sarah, money cannot buy."

"Listen," Joanne said, "they are announcing our flight. Let's hurry into the terminal." There weren't too many people on the flight, so we took our time boarding the plane, and in about an hour we reached Trinidad. We had plenty of time before we boarded our Air Canada flight to Toronto. We had left our suitcases in lockers at the airport so we collected them and went through customs early. It gave us time to browse through the duty-free shops and buy some Trinidadian rum. Finally, we boarded our flight for Toronto. It was a five-hour flight, so we got into Toronto airport around 6 o'clock that evening.

11

There was no lineup at customs so we got through in no time. David and Ramona were waiting for us. David drove Martha and myself home and Joanne and Sarah went with Ramona. We dropped Martha off first, and as we turned into our driveway, I saw Arshana peeping through the curtains.

When she saw that it was only David and I, she ran down the stairs and took my hand luggage. David brought up the suitcase. My feet were so swollen that I was barely able to walk up the stairs.

When I entered the living room, David pulled out a stool and said, "Now put your feet up." I raised my feet onto the stool and felt a lot better.

"Should I make you a cup of tea?" Arshana asked.

"Not at the moment," I said. "Let me relax for a while."

"You know," said David, "instead of looking rested, you look tired. How was the trip?"

"It was very nice, but I am getting far too old for these long trips. From now on I am going to spend my vacations in Canada and the USA."

I turned to Arshana, "Ask me where I went."

"Where did you go?" she asked. "To Guyana? You actually went to Guyana!"

"I certainly did, and I met your grandmother. Pass me my hand-bag."

From my handbag I took out the little box that held the chain and pendant. I gave it to her.

"Come on, open it," I said.

When she opened the box, her eyes lit up.

"You brought me an Aum." Her fingers hovered momentarily. She took the pendant and twisted and turned it in her hand.

"I've never seen anything so beautiful," she said. "Tell me, Mom, how you knew I wanted an Aum."

"The very first day I saw you, you were wearing an Aum around your neck."

"Someone stole it from me at Sita's place."

She continued to stare at the pendant, mystified. "This must have cost you a fortune. You should never have spent so much."

"Ram picked it out," I said.

"You met Uncle Ram?" she asked.

"I met him at the hotel and he took me to see your grandmother. I spent a few hours with her while the other ladies went to the falls. The next day, I introduced Ram to the other ladies and he acted as our guide until we left Guyana. He even took us to the airport. Arshana, all your grandmother's waking hours are spent thinking of you. She lives only for the day when you will return to Guyana."

She became silent. Tears were welling up in her eyes. She suddenly spun around and headed to the kitchen. I knew she went there to cry.

"David, did everything go well while I was away?"

"Nothing to complain about except that I had a bad case of the flu and had to stay in bed for a week. I went to work one day and collapsed. Dr. Taylor sent me home and told me to stay away until I was better. In fact, several other doctors also came down with the flu. To be honest, I didn't mind the little break at all. I had time to catch up on my reading.

"I didn't have a long time to enjoy my little vacation because I had to return to the office. A couple of new doctors joined our practice and we had to make quite a lot of adjustments to accommodate them. Dr. Taylor says everything must be in proper order before we leave in January. Dr. Fine will be given full responsibility to run the office in our absence."

"Oh are you going off then?"

"I suggested that I stay at the office when Dr. Taylor went on his next trip. But he said to me, 'Forget it David, Dr. Fine is quite capable and I do need you to come with me on this trip.'"

"Well, if he wants you to go," I said, "I don't think you have a choice. You should really go with him and at least see the place."

"Yes, I suppose I should, Mom. And I don't know about you, but I could do with a nice cup of tea."

"I could do with one myself."

Arshana had the kettle boiling, so she made us a cup of tea as soon as we entered the kitchen. When she poured the tea, I noticed that her hand shook.

"Are you not feeling well, Arshana? You look so pale," I said to her.

"Mom, I have been locked up in this place without fresh air or sunshine for three whole weeks. René would not allow me to leave the house."

"Who is talking about me?" René asked as he came walking through the kitchen door. "I just dropped my wife at the mall. So I took a quick spin over here to see if you had arrived," explained René.

"You'll never believe this, René, but I visited Arshana's home and met her grandmother."

"I don't believe it," René said jokingly. "Show me some proof."

"You want proof, René? I'll show you proof."

I turned to Arshana and asked her, "Arshana, would you mind dialing your grandmother's phone number for me, please?"

"I don't know it," she said.

"David, would you pass me my purse, please? The number is written in my address book."

David got the number from the address book and dialed it. He then handed the phone to Arshana and told her to speak to her grandmother. Reluctantly, she took the phone and I heard her say, "Is that you Tulsi? Tulsi this is Arshana."

"Arshana?" Tulsi's voice squeaked on the other end.

"Yes, it's Arshana. Can Grandma come to the phone?"

"She's right here," Tulsi said.

After a pause, we could all hear Auntie Lilly on the other end. "I can't hear," she said, "Peter is making so much noise. I think he heard your voice."

"Peter, Peter," Arshana called out. "Why are you making so much noise? And stop pulling grandma's hair. Now you better be quiet or Arshana will not love you anymore. I will put you in your cage and there will be no more papaya or coconut for you, understand?" She giggled into the phone. "Now, that's a good boy. I love you, Peter. And now let grandma speak."

A moment later, Arshana was speaking to her grandmother saying, "I know he misses me, and Grandma, I am here sitting with the lady from Canada who visited you a few days ago. She gave me the money you sent me. And Grandma, please don't cry. I promise you that as soon as I see the first snowfall, I'll return home to Guyana and I will never ever leave you again.

"Has Krishna been visiting you? …Oh, I am so sorry I missed him. I'm glad he comes to check on you every day. I must go now, Grandma. Don't cry. If you really want me to come home, I'll leave here tomorrow.

"Oh Grandma, as soon as I see the snow, I will return home. Don't cry, Grandma, please don't cry. I have to go now."

David replaced the phone and went to the living room. René stayed with Arshana, saying "I will always be here for you." She hugged him and then went to her room.

"So René, tell me," I said to him, "did everything go well in my absence?"

"Ma'am," René said, "this is the last time I will ever agree to a job like this. Before you left, you instructed me to keep the gate locked at all times. I did as you told me and only opened the gate for the doctor to go in and out. And because I listened to your instructions, I was cursed at and abused by all sorts of people.

"One day when the doctor was very ill, a young woman came to the gate. I told her that the doctor did not want any visitors. She called me a Spanish idiot and insisted that I open the gate. When I asked her to leave, she said 'I'll show you what I can do' and she tried to drive her car through the gate. Lucky you have a wrought iron gate and it stayed locked. I count my blessings that I was not standing in front of the gate either."

"René," I said, "I don't know what the doctor and I would do without you."

"You'll manage without me, Ma'am," he said. "I'm returning to El Salvador soon." Then he turned and walked out the kitchen door.

12

Sarah phoned a couple of weeks after we returned from vacation and invited me over to her house for lunch. "Ruth, I have something to discuss with you and I need your advice."

Sarah is a know-it-all. She would never ask for anyone's advice. I knew there was something really wrong, especially when I turned into the driveway and did not see Martha's car.

She looked worried, so before we sat down to lunch I said, "Sarah, out with it, the suspense is killing me. Tell me what you want to talk to me about."

"It's John. It has become impossible for me to live in the same house as him. I'm divorcing him."

"Why such a sudden decision?" I asked.

"It's not sudden, Ruth. We have been at each other's throats for a long time now. He claims that I always sided with the children instead of him. Ramona has been seeing someone who was married for some time now. His divorce is now final and he and Ramona want to get married right away. John adores Ramona, but he told her that if she wants to marry the divorcee, he wants nothing more to do with her.

"He told her that there are so many young and talented lawyers in the office and why couldn't she choose one of them? But Ramona told him that she was not interested in any of them and she has to be with Brian and no one else."

"Who is Brian? Do you know his family?"

"No, I don't. But everyone has heard about them. They are those Cohen people from George Street. They have three sons and Brian is the eldest. He was married to one of the Shulman girls," Sarah explained.

"Shulman?" I asked, "Where on Earth did I hear that name? Is one of those girls a dermatologist? I think David brought her over a couple of times."

"Yes, I believe two of the girls are doctors and Brian was married to the youngest one, who I believe is an architect," said Sarah.

She asked me, "Don't you remember reading about their million-dollar wedding in the society column? They dubbed it the wedding of the year. Well, guess what? The marriage lasted less than a year.

"Ramona handled Brian's divorce and I suppose that's how they met. Both Ramona and Brian want a very small, private wedding. Only immediate family and very close friends would be invited. Instead of having the reception in a large hotel, she's planning to ask you if she can use your party room.

"Ruth, please invite John over for dinner. You and David might be able to get the idea through his thick skull. Remember how he went berserk over your maid's roti and curry? I thought she had left for good but Cynthia said she's back at your house." Sarah was pleading.

"Sarah, I told you before that Arshana isn't a maid. She is someone who I enjoy having around my house. I've come to see her as a daughter. I have told you, Martha, and her miserable children to stop being mean to Arshana. A couple of days ago I had to ask Cynthia to leave my house, and I'm prepared to do so again if anyone insults her," I said firmly.

"Why are you so worked up, Ruth? I am so sorry," said Sarah.

"I get very angry, Sarah, when people choose to take advantage of an innocent person."

I took a moment to calm down, then asked, "Does John still work half days on Wednesdays, Sarah? Tomorrow is Wednesday and I can call him right now and find out if he's free."

"Whether he's free or not, Ruth, if you invite him, he will come."

"You never know, he could have something planned for tomorrow."

"Leave it to me, Ruth. Let me handle this."

"As you wish."

Seemingly satisfied with our conversation, Sarah relaxed a bit, then said, "Oh, Ruth, we were talking so much that I forgot I invited you for lunch! I made a casserole. Let's have it with a bottle of wine."

Sarah always made good casseroles, and this one was delicious. She made it with tuna and cheese. After lunch I told Sarah I would see her tomorrow and left.

Sarah phoned early the next morning to say that she and John would be over at my house no later than six. She wasn't kidding. At 6 o'clock on the dot, she and John walked into the house.

"You look great, Ruth," John said as he hugged me. "I don't believe I have seen you since you returned from holidays. I heard you girls had a good time."

Without waiting for an answer, he looked over my shoulder and said, "Oh, the dinner table is already set up. I am famished; I had no lunch because I knew I was coming here."

"Well, dinner is ready. We can eat right now if you'd like," I said.

"Not before I have something to drink," Sarah said. And to David she said, "You haven't kissed your aunt Sarah or offered her a drink."

"I was just waiting for you to sit down and get comfortable," David replied.

"Stop making excuses, give me a hug and bring me the usual."

"Same for you, Uncle John?" David asked.

"Well if we must drink before dinner, sure," John responded.

David brought them both scotch and sodas and Arshana appeared at the same time with the dish of codfish cakes.

"Oh, they look and smell so good," said John. "I'm going to try a few of them. But first you come here, young lady and give Uncle John a kiss."

Arshana hesitated and then looked towards me for approval.

When she saw me smile, she went and kissed John on his cheek.

"I heard you left," John said.

"Oh, she did leave," I said. "But I begged her to come back. Eleanor had to return to Paris and I am trying to persuade Arshana to stay with me until she returns to Guyana."

"Do you have to go back to Guyana?" John asked.

"Yes, I'm here only on a visitor's visa," Arshana explained.

"Well, if you want to stay, let me know. But my guess is that a beautiful young woman like you would have tons of young men waiting for you at home," John said. "And now I'm ready to eat."

After the food was put on the table, John said to Arshana, "Now come here young lady, you must sit and eat with us."

"I am not hungry, Uncle John. Let me bring some more food for you."

"Oh, I'll help myself. I'm not accustomed to such good food or service at home."

"There is one thing I can say," Sarah said, "Arshana is not dumb. She knows the way to a man's heart is through his stomach."

"This young lady doesn't need to get to a man's heart through his stomach. She is a piece of gold. She's of the finest quality. I wonder where women like her were hiding 40 years ago."

"Probably hiding from you," Sarah said. "And I was the idiot to find you."

Things always ended with John and Sarah fighting through dinner, so David, in order to change the subject, said to John, "Uncle John, I have a very special wine that I would like you to try."

"Thank you David, but no more drinks for me tonight, not even coffee." He then got up from the dinner table and said, "Ruth, I have enjoyed your dinner. You know I always do. And right now I am tempted to go sit in my favorite chair and relax, but I won't. If I do so, I will never be able to get up.

"So now tell me, Ruth, why did you invite me here tonight? I'm sure it isn't because of my good looks. Sarah told you to invite me."

I didn't respond.

"It's about Ramona, isn't it?" said John. "All I have to say is that Ramona is no longer a child. I cannot tell her what she should or should not do, but as my daughter, I still have the right to advise her. Her choice of a husband isn't what I had expected. She's a good lawyer and one of the brightest in her field. She has a promising future ahead of her, but I fear that there is no doubt that marrying Brian would harm her success."

"What gives you the right to judge Brian for his mistakes?" Sarah glowered at him. "And from what I heard, his situation was not his fault."

"I have nothing more to say about this," said John, and he walked towards the door. Then he stood in the doorway, turned back and said, "Are you coming along, Sarah? Honestly, I'd rather you didn't. Oh, by the way David, I am off next Wednesday and I would like to invite this young lady to dinner."

Arshana was standing not too far away.

"Where would you like us to meet you?" David asked.

"Us? I didn't ask you to come, David."

"David," Sarah said, "this old goat would certainly like to be seen with a young woman, but I've got news for him. He is stuck with me for life unless I decide to free him."

John said, "Believe me, Sarah, you haven't had any control over me for a long time," and he walked through the door and down the stairs.

13

"Auntie Ruth, Auntie Ruth, where are you?" Ramona's voice resounded through the house.

"In the kitchen, Ramona."

Preparations for the wedding were underway. When Ramona walked into the kitchen, she said, "Hi Auntie Ruth. Hi Arshana. I believe you were all still asleep when I let in the florist this morning. I am so pleased with the work she did. Just awesome. The entire room is filled with forget-me-nots and lilies of the valley. Go and see for yourself. You won't recognize it. There are a few things that I still have to do, but I wouldn't mind a cup of tea before I go."

Arshana plugged in the kettle and made Ramona a cup of tea. As she sipped her tea, she said, "I have told everyone to be here around 6 o'clock. "If I'm not here, could you ask David to receive the guests for me? And Arshana, I am looking forward to seeing you."

"Ramona, I don't like parties," Arshana said.

"Oh really? Are you going to insult me by not showing up at my party? If I don't see you downstairs tonight, I'll be up to get you. Anyways, I have to go now," she said, and ran through the kitchen door.

"Arshana," I said, "Ramona has always been very nice to you. So many times I heard her yell at her mother if she said anything distasteful about you. You shouldn't disappoint her. You would look beautiful in the red dress we bought at Monique's."

Leaving her to think things over, I went upstairs to grab a few drinks.

Soon enough, it was a quarter to six; time to get ready for the party. I took a quick shower, got dressed and went straight to Arshana's room. She was dressed, but she stood in her usual place, staring out the window.

"Are you coming downstairs?" I asked.

"I don't want to go."

"Why not, Arshana?"

"Because I am tired of being ridiculed."

"Arshana, this is my house. If I hear anyone making disparaging remarks about you, I'll deal with them. Please, at least do this for Ramona. Now you go on and finish getting ready."

Just then, I heard David in the hall, apparently looking for us.

"Mom, Mom, where are you?"

"I'm in Arshana's room."

He rapped on the door and then came in.

"What is going on?" he asked, "Almost everyone is here. Brian's parents have arrived and even Auntie Martha and Auntie Sarah are here, and they are never on time."

"We're ready, but I am still trying to convince Arshana to come to the party."

"Arshana," David said quietly.

She slowly turned from the window. Her eyes filled with tears. She looked beautiful in the red dress. I could see that David, or any man, for that matter, would be smitten with her.

"Arshana," David said, "I've already seen all the girls down at the party and trust me, not one of them is as pretty as you are. Now, with those beautiful brown eyes, give us a smile and let's see those dimples."

She smiled in a perfectly polite way.

"That's better," David said. He then held her hand and led us out of the room.

"Aren't I lucky?" he said. "I am escorting two of the most beautiful ladies to the party."

All the tables were occupied. The only one that was available was the one next to Sarah and Martha. David sensed that neither Arshana nor I wanted to sit there, but we had no choice, and to make matters worse, Eric was sitting at their table. David pulled out chairs, told us to sit and went to the bar to get us drinks.

I saw Martha give Sarah a nudge, but I pretended not to notice.

Just then, Ken Campbell saw us from his place at the bar. He came over to our table and said, "Hello Mrs. Weissman, hello Arshana. Can I join you ladies?"

"Certainly, Ken," I said.

At the same time, David returned with a Coke for Arshana and a champagne cocktail for me.

"David, what's the matter with you?" asked Ken. "Is your lady still drinking Coke? When I marry her, the very first thing I'm going to do is teach her to drink."

"Good luck," David said.

"Auntie Ruth, Auntie Ruth," Eric said as he leaned over towards my table. "I wonder how much money Ramona is paying those jokers over there."

"What are you talking about Eric?"

"The musicians. I haven't heard a sound from them yet."

"They're probably waiting for people to settle down, Eric."

"Well I'm settled, and I intend to let them know." Then he shouted to the singer, "You, you over there, sing me an Elvis Presley song."

"Which one would you like to hear?" the singer asked.

"Love Me Tender," Eric replied. The pianist sat at his bench and the singer began the song.

Two couples got on the floor and began to dance. Eric also got up and came stumbling over to our table. Both Ken and David were watching him. They knew he was going to come over and ask Arshana to dance, so David got up and asked her first.

Martha then leaned over to my table and said, "Ruth, I thought you had sent that girl away. Do you think your David is immune to her manipulation?"

"He's just trying to protect her," I said.

"A girl like her doesn't need protection."

"Martha, Arshana did not want to come to the party. Ask Ramona, she'll tell you."

"Ruth, don't avoid my questions. Why is she still here?"

"Eleanor had to return to Paris. She begged me to keep Arshana once again and I did. We missed her when she went away; René, David and myself. I plan to let her stay with me until she returns to Guyana."

"And when is that?" Martha asked.

"I don't know. And I do hope that it won't be before Christmas."

When the song was over and the music stopped, David and Arshana returned to the table.

Cynthia, who was sitting with her mother, staggered over to the table, falling on Ken's lap.

"Sorry," she said, "I meant to fall on his lap." She pointed at David. "Now get up," she said to him, "go and bring me a drink, David."

"You know where the bar is, Cynthia. And you don't need another drink," David said.

"Mind your own business," she said. "I'll show you!"

She got up from the chair and jumped onto David's lap.

"Stop bouncing on me, you're not exactly a lightweight, you know." David looked annoyed, "Auntie Martha, could you ask this spoiled brat of yours to behave herself?"

Martha shrugged, "I couldn't control the two of you when you were kids and I don't intend to do it now."

Naomi, a tall blonde who worked with Cynthia, came over to our table and said, "Are you two fooling around or dancing?" And to David, she said, "Why don't you ever ask me to dance? I have to ask you all the time."

"Naomi, believe me, I was tempted to come over and ask you for a dance but I was scared of all the handsome young men that you have around you."

"Get lost, Naomi," Cynthia said. "He's dancing with me first."

"May I have your attention, please, everyone!" It was Ramona at the mic. "Dinner is ready. I know you are going to love what we've prepared for you. Enjoy!" she said.

As folks were heading towards the buffet table, I noticed that John walked past the table, took a quick look and walked in our direction. When he reached our table, I said "Aren't you eating, John?"

"To be honest, Ruth, nothing on the table appeals to me. I'm not a big fan of seafood."

And turning to Arshana, he said, "Young lady, why don't you make some good food? I'll bet you $100 that you can't cook me some curry and roti in 15 minutes."

"I can't lose a bet like that," promised Arshana.

Ken chirped up suddenly, "Did I hear someone mention curry?"

"You have sharp ears, Ken," I said. And to Arshana I said, "Take Uncle John and Mr. Campbell upstairs and give them some food."

I explained to the men, "She was cooking up a storm this morning and I am sure she made some curry."

Arshana was more than happy to leave the party. She hurried up the stairs with John and Ken following closely behind her.

Half an hour later, John returned and he said, "Ruth, I am so stuffed. I'd like to go to bed."

"So would I," Ken said.

Arshana returned 15 minutes later, having cleaned the kitchen, and said to John, who was sitting at our table, "Pay up, Mr. Nadler, you lost your bet."

"Pay the lady, John," Ken said. "I was sitting right here at this table next to Mrs. Weissman when you made that bet."

"Yes, I lost," agreed John.

He took out his wallet, opened it, took out a hundred dollar bill and handed it to Arshana.

"Please Mr. Nadler, I was only joking. I could never take your money," laughed Arshana.

"But I could," David said.

"Oh, no, come here young lady," said John, and he kissed Arshana on her cheek.

"Ruth," Martha said, "Did you see what I just saw or am I too drunk? Did you see the way John kissed that girl?"

Even Sarah mentioned how outrageous it was. "Sarah, Martha," I said, "Please stop picking on Arshana. From day one, both of you have been very cruel to her. It has to stop. John treats her like his daughter."

"Those were no fatherly kisses he gave her," said Martha.

"Martha, you are drunk," I said.

Eric was sitting next to his mother and he heard her remarks and said to John, "Uncle John, I didn't think I would live to see the day."

"What do you mean?" asked John.

Eric continued, "Are you paying for certain services?"

Ken, who was still sitting at our table, got up and said to Eric, "If you weren't so drunk, I would've knocked you to the ground."

David touched Ken on the shoulder and said "Let me handle this." And to Eric he said, "You have been an idiot and a nuisance all night. I don't permit anyone to be disrespectful to a guest in my house and if there is any further trouble from you, I'll throw you out the door myself."

The incident went unnoticed by most of the drunk, dancing crowd, but Arshana overheard everything. She asked me if she could leave. David saw the tears in her eyes and he took her hand and asked her to dance.

"That girl has won," Cynthia said to me. "The singer is singing Spanish Eyes. David knows that is my favorite song and instead of dancing with me, he chose to dance with that dirty little Trini."

"Cynthia," I said, "If I were you, I would be more careful with what I say. David is already very angry with your brother."

"Excuse my language, Auntie Ruth, but what the hell could David do to me?"

Lyle Nadler and his fiancée Jenny had come over to talk to us and had overheard what Cynthia had said. Lyle told her, "Both you and Eric have had far too much to drink. I suggest that both of you just go home."

"Don't lecture me, Lyle," Cynthia said. "I suggest you concentrate on that snake you plan on marrying."

Jenny heard her but pretended that she didn't. "Auntie Ruth, I am wearing my bracelets," she said, trying to make light conversation about the bracelets that her mother, Joanne, had brought from Guyana.

"They are so beautiful, Jenny," I said.

"Auntie Ruth, you wouldn't believe all the compliments I receive when I wear them."

"Oh, I believe you."

David and Arshana finished a dance and returned to our table at that moment, followed by Ramona.

"Auntie Ruth," Ramona said, "Is the party OK? Do you think everyone is having a good time? Brian's dad seems to be enjoying the party. I hope my mother and Auntie Martha aren't making fools of themselves in front of Brian's mother."

"Don't worry," I said, "Brian's mom looks like a really understanding woman."

"David, aren't you going to ask me to dance?" Ramona asked.

"I'd like nothing better, but Brian is looking in your direction and I wouldn't want him to punch me."

"Well you'll have to take your chances, buddy, dance with me."

"I think your father is coming over to the table. Maybe he wants to dance with you," said David. But John passed David and Ramona and went over to Arshana and asked her to dance.

"I don't want to dance, Uncle John," she said.

"Don't let these idiots bring you down," he whispered. "They're just jealous."

While John was saying this, David went over to the singer and asked him to sing Oh My Papa, then David and Ramona came to our table. David said to John, "I'd like to change partners."

John hesitated for a moment, then he threw his arms around his daughter and hugged her. Ramona began to cry and John took out his handkerchief from his pocket and wiped her eyes.

"When she was a little girl, I could never say no to her, and now that she's grown up, nothing has changed. She will always be my little girl," John said, in a husky voice. And to Brian, who was standing close by, he said, "If you ever hurt a hair on her head, I'll throttle you."

Then John asked the band to play Ramona's favorite song, Ramona by The Waterfalls and he danced with his daughter. A few couples got up and began to dance. Eric got up from his chair, came over to where Arshana was sitting and said, "You're dancing this one with me."

"Don't even try it," Ken warned Eric. "Go and dance with someone as drunk as you are. Leave this lady alone."

"Who said she was a lady? She's not in our class," Eric said.

Ken got up, held Eric by his collar and said, "Another word from you and I'll knock you to the ground."

David was talking to Brian's dad and when he heard Ken's voice, he strode over to our table. "What's going on?" he asked Ken.

"David, I'm leaving. If I stay any longer, I'll get myself in trouble. Ramona is dancing and I don't want to disturb her, so I would appreciate it if you thanked her on my behalf for inviting me," said Ken.

David understood. "I'll walk you out," he said. Then to Arshana he said, "You better go upstairs."

Shortly afterwards later, David returned, and Cynthia, who was sitting at our table, went up to him and asked, "Did you put the little tramp to bed?"

"Cynthia, both you and your brother are disgusting and disrespectful. Look at him," he said, pointing to Eric, "Look at him annoying that poor woman at the bar."

"My brother can smell a tramp anywhere. I can't say the same for you, David."

There was a loud noise and when I looked towards the bar I saw Eric sprawled on the floor. The woman was not going to put up with any of Eric's nonsense. Apparently, she had told him to leave her alone several times and when he refused to stop, she turned around and kicked him in the groin.

That did it. The incident brought the party to an end, and soon enough, everyone left.

"No more parties in this house," I said to David. "I don't know what your father was thinking when he built this huge party room. No parties ever again. Never." I sighed. "David, I'm very tired, I'm going to bed. You can lock up the house."

When I got to my room and into bed, I could not sleep. I twisted and turned for a while and then decided to go to the kitchen for some milk. I poured the milk, heated it up in the microwave for a few seconds and drank it all in one gulp. I hoped the warm milk would induce sleep.

As I was returning to my room, I heard voices coming from Arshana's room. I knew she always slept with the radio on but I could have sworn I heard David's voice. No, it couldn't be. All that champagne was making me hear things.

When I got into bed again, it still took me a while to fall asleep but when I did, it was a deep sleep.

14

Sunlight peeped through the opening in the drapes, waking me up. I looked at my watch, it was almost 11. I slowly got out of bed, went to the bathroom, brushed my teeth, threw on my housecoat over my nightgown and went down to the kitchen. From the traces of egg left on the plate in the kitchen, I knew that David had already eaten breakfast. He stood with Arshana by the window, his arms around her waist. I pretended not to notice.

"Sleep well, Mom?" David asked, hugging me. He pulled out a chair for me.

"I just had breakfast," Arshana said. "Want me to make your favorite cheese omelette?"

"Sure, I'm very hungry."

While she made me the omelettes, David poured me some coffee and made me a couple of slices of toast.

"Any more problems after I went to bed last night?" I asked.

"Just a bit with Uncle Carl and Eric. Uncle Carl took away Eric's car keys and wouldn't allow him to drive home."

"Eric needs help," I said.

"The only person who can help Eric is himself," David said.

"What shall I prepare for lunch?" Arshana asked.

"Lunch?" I asked. "I am eating lunch right now. I don't think I want anything else to eat until dinnertime."

"So what are we having for dinner?" Arshana continued.

"I don't know, we'll think of something when I get home. After breakfast, I'm going to visit a friend of mine," I said.

"I'm not going to be home until late in the afternoon," David said.

"Mom, since no one is around," Arshana said, "can I go and visit my friends?"

"Certainly, and there is plenty of food from last night's party. Why don't you take some?" I said.

"There's nothing downstairs anymore. The caterers were here very early this morning. They cleaned up the place and took everything," Arshana said.

"But there is still plenty of food in the fridge, get rid of it all. It will only go to waste."

"Thank you, Mom, I will."

Half an hour later, when I was dressed and ready to leave, I still saw her fussing around in the kitchen.

"If you were ready," I said, "I could've given you a ride."

"No thank you, Mom. David also offered me a ride but I am not going very far from here and it is such a nice day; a walk in the park would be so refreshing."

"As you wish," I said, leaving the house.

My friend Annie had had several eye operations. Some of them were unsuccessful, so she never drove anymore. She had been my friend since high school and she looked forward to my visits. Annie lived just a stone's throw away from the Erin Mills Town Centre. I needed to do some shopping, so I decided to stop at the mall and pick up a pair of gloves before going over to Annie's. The mall was not very crowded. I found a shop that sold gloves and winter accessories.

I bought a pair of gloves for myself and a pair for Arshana and a hat and scarf to match. As I was leaving, I noticed that the shop just opposite had coats on sale. I remember that Arshana only had the light coat I had bought her. It was a dressy coat, so I went into the store and bought a heavier one. When I paid for the coat, I glanced at my watch and realized that I had spent far too much time shopping. I didn't want to waste any more time so I picked up a cake from one of the bakeries in the mall and headed over to Annie's.

Annie was delighted to see me.

"Oh Ruth," she said, "I thought you had forgotten about me."

"You know I'll never do that. It's just that the days seem to go by so quickly."

"Maybe for you, Ruth, because you are busy. For me, the days are long and boring."

"Let me put the kettle on," I said.

I made us both some tea, and we ate some cake and chatted for a while. Eventually I told Annie that I had to go.

"Not so soon, Ruth."

"It's Friday, Annie. I don't want to get caught up in the rush hour traffic. But I'll make you a promise; on my next visit I'll spent more time with you. And now let me give you a hug."

As I hugged her, I saw tears in her eyes and I felt so sorry.

I got home just in time to beat the traffic. Arshana was already home and cooking something in the oven.

"What are you cooking? I was planning on ordering Chinese food tonight."

"Oh, I'm not cooking," she said, "I'm making a baked custard. You ate it in Guyana and you told me how much you liked it.

"We all liked it, especially Joanne. She had it at every meal. And now would you sit down and let me show you my purchases?"

When she saw what I had bought, she said, "Thank you so much Mom, but you are wasting your money. I can never wear these things in Guyana."

"You can always give them to your friends when you leave," I said.

"Anyone at home?" called René.

"We're in the kitchen, René," I said.

"I just dropped that witch in the mall," he said. "I noticed that tulip bulbs were on sale so I bought you some. Though I doubt I will be here next year to plant them. I'm going to El Salvador after the Christmas holidays and I'm not planning on returning.

"I like being in Canada and I like working for you, Ma'am, but the time has come and I must make a decision. If I continue to stay with my wife, I'll end up with a heart attack. She is only interested in the money I give her. When you were away and the doctor had the flu, he was miserable; though I guess I don't have to tell you how he gets when he's sick.

"Anyways, some days I stayed on a little longer to keep Miss Arshana company. And then there was a break-in, two doors down, at the O'Neill's house. The police discovered that it was an inside job. The maid let her boyfriend in and he burglarized the place. I wasn't taking any chances. I slept over in my room downstairs to guard the place. Some evenings, if I tried to go home instead, my wife would throw a coffee cup at me and hit me in the face.

"'Where were you last evening?' she would ask. 'I waited and waited for you to take me shopping and you never came home.'

"I told her about the burglary. And she always claims to be a decent Catholic, but you know what she said? She went down on her knees and said, 'please Lord, please let the burglars get him and beat the daylights out of him'. That's the sort of church-going woman I have to deal with every day of my life."

"She really didn't mean what she said, René," I said.

"Oh, she meant it alright. I can tell you this, Ma'am, had it not been for you, I would've left this country long ago, but you have been very kind and very generous to me for 30 years. Of course, I cannot forget all the good things that Mr. Solomon did for me as well.

"I watched Dr. David grow from a small boy to a young man, and eventually into a doctor. He never gave me any problems. He was always obedient and respectful... but now he's making up for all those trouble-free days and years. Last Saturday he went to the casino in Niagara Falls, and the next day a young lady came to the gate. From the words that came out of her mouth, I can tell you she was no lady.

"You will remember, this is the second time a crazy woman has come to the gate and yelled at me to let her in. At least she did not try to drive through the gate. Flossy was standing next to me so I told her that if she didn't leave, I'd let Flossy out. That got rid of her. After she left, she must have called the doctor and complained, because five minutes later, the doctor invited me upstairs for a brandy. Oh, I can hear his car, let me run and open the gate for him."

"You stay right here, René. The doctor needs some exercise. He's putting on weight. It's Arshana's cooking. Even I have gained weight."

"Me too," René said.

David came striding up the stairs and as he entered the kitchen he asked, "What's for dinner? I'm starving."

"Chinese," I said.

"Order it now, I'm hungry," said David.

"I'll leave now, Ma'am," René said.

"Why don't you stay and have dinner with us?"

"I'd like nothing better, Ma'am, but I have to pick up the witch. If I'm late, she will raise hell. Chinese food tastes better the next day. Put my share in the fridge for tomorrow," said René, then he said his goodbyes and left.

The next day, I was sitting at the kitchen table having a nice cup of tea when David came in. He was just finishing up a phone call. "That was Uncle John," he said.

"Last week I gave him a few documents that Dr. Taylor's lawyer wanted Dr. Taylor to sign. Uncle John read them over and said everything was legitimate but he would still like to propose a few minor changes. He will be stopping by tonight on his way home from work and asked if that pretty young lady would be around. He said that if she will, he expects her to make his favorite dish. I know there's no pretty young lady in this house. I wonder whom he meant."

Then David looked at his watch. "I'm up to my eyeballs with appointments and I'm late."

He gave me a quick hug, pulled Arshana's ponytail and said, "Don't get carried away, Uncle John didn't mean you." She chuckled after him. It felt good to watch them getting along so well.

"Off to work," I said, pushing him through the door. "And don't run. The steps are wet and slippery."

After he left, I went downstairs to the freezer and brought up some chicken and red snapper. "Make the snapper the Guyanese way," I said to Arshana. "Sarah has a German maid now and John isn't too keen on her cooking. He eats a heavy lunch downtown and barely touches whatever she gives him for supper.

"Arshana? Why don't you let Uncle John help you to get an extension on your visa? You can stay at least until the spring."

"Several people have told me that if you want to stay in Canada, stay and hide. But never go into immigration for an extension. But Mom, when I arrived in Canada, I was given permission to stay until the fifteenth of January so I will remain until then or maybe even leave before that. When I return to Guyana, I will apply at the Canadian embassy in the proper and legal way. If I need your help, and I am pretty sure I will, I will phone and ask.

"Last week I spoke to my grandmother. She's very ill and she promised me that she would not die in peace until I get home. I don't want to worry her."

"Arshana," I said, "I can see that you've already made up your mind to return to Guyana. But we would all miss you, especially René."

"Who is talking about me?" René asked as he came through the kitchen door.

He pulled out a chair and sat down.

"René, you always show up when we are talking about you. But you don't seem like your usual self. Is something wrong?" I asked.

"Plenty Ma'am, plenty. My mother-in-law is here and I'm not returning home until she leaves. I hope you wouldn't mind if I stay in my room downstairs."

"Solomon built that room for you, René. As far as I'm concerned you can stay there forever. And I know that Arshana would love to have you in the kitchen all the time," I said.

"Why not?" Arshana said, "and he can begin by passing me a couple of lemons."

Then Arshana said to me, "Mom, you said earlier today that you had to write down some cheques. You also told me yesterday that Rabbi Newman would be coming over today. You wanted me to remind you. Why don't you go and write your cheques? René is here. He can help me with the cooking."

Rabbi Newman arrived shortly thereafter and stayed much longer than I had expected. After he left, I went upstairs and took a quick shower. I was barely finished when I heard John's voice in the living room.

"Hi John," I said, kissing him on the cheek. "Long time no see."

"You wouldn't imagine how busy I've been lately. Plenty of work, but very little money. And now where is my little girl?" John asked as he made his way towards the kitchen.

Arshana heard his voice and she came out to greet him.

"Hi Uncle John," she said. She hugged him and took his briefcase.

"I would give my right arm to have a greeting like this every day when I get home. And now I'm so hungry. If dinner is ready, let's eat first and talk business afterwards," John said.

"David, I am ashamed to say this, but I have not been in the kitchen all afternoon. Is dinner ready?" I asked.

"Of course," said David.

"Rabbie Newman was here and you know what he's like," I explained to John.

"How much did he rip you off?" asked John.

"Uncle John," David interrupted, "would you like a scotch before dinner, or would you prefer some wine with your meal?"

"I'll have a scotch, thanks."

"Same for you, Mom?"

"Yes please."

"Girl," John said to Arshana, "why don't you sit down and eat?"

"I want to serve you, Uncle John. Do you like fish?"

"I love fish," John said.

"Then give me your plate." Arshana placed a whole fish on his plate and carefully removed the bones. "Tell me if you like fish cooked this way better."

"It smells delicious," John said, picking up a piece of fish with his fork and putting it in his mouth, closing his eyes to savour the taste.

"Sarah loves fish prepared this way too," I said.

"She has a pair of hands," John said, "she can learn to cook it this way if she wants to."

John sighed with satisfaction, he was enjoying the meal. "I've already eaten a whole fish and I still see more on the platter. So now I have a big problem."

"Let me help you decide, Uncle John," said Arshana. She bent down and whispered something in his ear and filleted another fish for him.

After dinner, John said, "I would really like a coffee and brandy to finish up this excellent meal, but I would prefer to go over these papers first."

John and David were left to do the paperwork whilst René and I cleared the table and helped Arshana with the dishes. Less than half an hour later, John yelled, "Girl, Uncle John is ready for his coffee."

"Got everything straightened out, John?" I asked.

"I hope so, Ruth. Dr. Taylor's lawyers are some of the best in the business. I'm sure they wouldn't mind a couple of changes. You know, one of these days, your son is going to be a very rich man. I hope he remembers his poor Uncle John when he makes the Forbes list."

David said, "I make a comfortable living and Dad made some good investments for Mom and I. We have more than enough money to live on. With the way the economy is going these days, not even the so-called pundits could predict the future."

"Are you busy in the office these days, John?" I asked.

"I'm always busy. But these days I'm not in court very much. I am now doing most of the administrative work in our office. Joseph Steen was in charge of that side of the business but he had two heart attacks, one after the other, so he rarely comes to the office anymore. I swear, everyone is getting heart attacks and I feel like I'm going to be the next victim.

"And Ruth, before I forget again, over the years our office would normally celebrate both Christmas and Hanukkah in October. Usually it's only for members of our staff. But we had a really good year, so after getting the approval of the other senior partners, I am going to have a hell of a party.

"I'm asking staff members, their spouses or partners or whatever, some relatives and a few preferred clients. As you know, I've been meaning to ask the young lady out to dinner for some time now, so I am now inviting both of you to the party. David, I suppose I have no choice but to invite you too. And if you don't mind, I'd like my brandy now."

David got up and poured John his drink.

"By the way," said John, "the holiday party is usually a black-tie affair. And now before I go, I'm going to the kitchen to thank that little lady for the fantastic dinner and personally invite her to the party... Oh there she is."

Arshana walked into the living room holding a paper bag.

"This is for your dinner tomorrow night, Uncle John," and she handed him the bag.

"Thank you," John said. "Promise me that I will see you at my party in a couple of weeks."

David saw John off and he came back to the kitchen and said, "I hope you heard what Uncle John said. A black-tie event means long dresses for both of you."

"Thanks and no thanks to Arshana's cooking," I said, "I have put on so much weight that I doubt any of my long dresses will fit me. Tomorrow Arshana and I are making a trip over to Monique's. She is sure to have lots of new dresses in for Christmas."

"I don't need a dress. I am not going to the party," Arshana said.

"You can't disappoint Uncle John," I said. "As long as I can remember, John has had his annual office party, and not once has he invited either me or David. I think he did so this year because he wants to invite you. It is his way of saying 'thank you' for all the dinners you have made him."

"If he is happy because of the dinners I have made him, I am glad, but I want nothing in return. I am not going to the party."

"René," David said, "Don't you think it is wrong for her to refuse Uncle John's invitation?"

"Pardon me, sir, she has every right to refuse it if she doesn't want to go. She loves this Mr. Nadler. It is the others who humiliate and belittle her all the time. Many times, I have heard her being insulted. She has just as many feelings as anyone else."

"René, don't encourage her. I was expecting some help from you," David said.

"I am not encouraging her, sir, but she is in no position to stand up and defend herself every time. It hurts me to see her cry. But I promise you, sir, and I mean it, if anyone insults her in my presence, whether it is a man or woman, they will get a punch in the face. You and madam can fire me afterwards."

"René, do you think anyone would dare say anything to her in my presence?" asked David.

"Pardon me again, sir, where were you when that drunken bum grabbed her at Miss Ramona's party? What did you do about it? From that night onwards, Ken Campbell will always be respected by me. He defended her."

"I was ready to go downstairs and beat the crap out of that bastard but Ken and Arshana begged me not to."

"René," Arshana said as she threw her arms around him and hugged him. "Thank you for standing up for me, but you must never forget that in the eyes of some people, we are only hired help." Tears streamed down her face but she made no effort to dry them.

"Good night," she said and walked towards her room.

15

It was the night of the party and hundreds of stars lit up the sky. But when I threw open my bedroom window, a gust of cold air blasted through.

Winter was just around the corner. Realizing that both Arshana and I would need something warm to wrap around our shoulders, I went to my closet and took out two pashmina shawls.

Then I went to Arshana's room and found her already dressed.

When she saw me, she made a brave attempt to smile but the look in her eyes revealed that something was terribly wrong.

Before I had the chance to ask her what was wrong, David rapped on the door and came into the room. He was speechless when he saw how stunning she looked, but he also realized that something was wrong.

"What's the matter? Don't you want to go to the party?" he asked.

"I had hoped that you and Mom would have understood my reasons for not wanting to go," said Arshana. "There will be some people at the party who don't like me. They'll taunt and insult me all night long." She began to cry.

"I understand how you feel Arshana," I said.

"No you don't, Mom."

"Arshana, if John didn't ask you himself, I would have told you not to go. So I'm making a promise to you right now, that if anyone dares insult you, we will leave the party immediately," I said.

"Arshana," David said, "Don't you think that people will gossip about Mom and I too? Who cares? Now dry those tears, give us a smile and let us go to the kitchen so René can see how beautiful you look."

René was startled when Arshana walked into the kitchen.

"Is that really you, Miss Arshana? I wish I had my camera here tonight. Trust me, no one else at the party will look as beautiful as you. In fact, where is my wallet?"

René found his wallet, opened it, took out a $50 bill and placed it on the table. "Sir," he said to David, "I'm going to make a bet that there won't be another young lady at the party as pretty as Miss Arshana."

"René," I said, "You are always betting and as far as I can remember, I have never seen you win. But you have a sure winner here tonight. Double it. Make it $100."

"Come on," David said. "We don't want to be late."

And to René he said, "I'll make sure that I check out all the pretty girls at the party and I'll give you the results in the morning. You know I have an eye for pretty ladies."

"Oh please don't remind me, sir. I'm trying to forget all the headaches that you have given me over the years. Now let me run and open the gate. Smile, Ms. Arshana, smile, have fun," René said as we drove off.

The restaurant was only 15 minutes away from my house, so we got there in no time. The parking lot was jam-packed but David gave his keys to the valet and we walked in.

"Is this place always so crowded, David?" I asked.

"Even during the week," he replied. "It is always difficult to get a reservation here. I believe the owner is a client of Uncle John's, which is why he got this place."

John was apparently looking out for us, because as soon as we entered the restaurant, he greeted us.

As he was leading us to our table, Francesco the owner came towards us smiling.

"Dr. Weissman," he said, "I came to your office last week to see you and Dr. Taylor but I was told you were in a meeting and Dr. Taylor was in India."

"Dr. Taylor will be back next week," David said.

"Are you Johnny's guest, Dr. Weissman?"

"Yes they are," John said, "And I have the pleasure of escorting these two beautiful ladies to their seats."

As we were led to our table, I saw several people staring at us.

Arshana was wearing a turquoise blue silk dress. It clung to her shapely body, displaying every curve. Antonio, my hairdresser, had done a fantastic job with her hair. He had swept it all back and put it high on her head. He finished off by placing two Diamante pins on the sides of her head. They matched perfectly with the glittering diamante belt on her dress. She looked like a Roman goddess.

When we were seated, John told us to order whatever we wanted to drink. Arshana sat between David and I. Ramona and Brian sat next to David. Cynthia, Eric and Lyle sat with their partners at our table also. Martha, Sarah and Joanne sat at the next table with their spouses and the senior partners from their office.

I felt Martha and Sarah's eyes on me but I refused to look in their direction.

"I don't believe this!" Arshana said. Her face went from shock to disbelief to amazement and finally, joy. "Vish," she asked, "Are you a waiter? Shouldn't you be in medical school?"

"Shana, is that you? What are you doing here? I am so shocked, I can hardly speak. And to answer your question, I am in medical school. I am studying at McGill in Montréal. I have just finished my exams. I came to Toronto for a break. I have been in Trenton for almost two weeks. I am returning to Montréal tomorrow. Shana, Franco and I did everything we could to find you. Franco's dad owns this place and we work here when we're in Toronto. Franco and I share a room in Montréal and I stay at his house when I'm in Toronto.

"Now, let me take the orders."

David and I ordered scotch and Arshana got a coke.

"Still drinking Coke, Shana? Grandma isn't around to watch, if that's what you think, even if I feel her eyes on me all the time."

Five minutes later, Vish returned with our drinks, accompanied by a smiling young man who he introduced to us as Francesco 'Franco' Junior.

"Shana," Franco said, "as soon as we returned from Guyana, we moved heaven and earth to find you. Where are you staying? Unfortunately, we're returning to Montréal tomorrow, but we're going to take your phone number."

The three Guyanese looked over-joyed to have met one another.

Arshana had stars in her eyes and had never looked so happy.

"In August we were in Guyana and we had the time of our lives," continued Franco. "Every morning we would go over to your grandma's house and Tulsi would prepare whatever we wanted for breakfast. Vish and I are planning to return to Guyana just after reading week, but my parents want me to go to Italy instead.

"I'll take you over to meet my mom a little later. Vish and I have told her a lot about you. She is sitting across the room with her relatives visiting from Italy. If there's anything you want, just tell Vish, he is in charge of your table. I am working at the other end of the room."

"I am sure Vish will look after us," Arshana said, "you go and serve your table."

A few minutes later, Vish appeared with a basket of Italian delicacies and a bottle of wine.

"Franco's mama sent it for you. Look, she is waving. Franco will take you over to the table later," Vish told Arshana.

David took up the bottle of wine, leaned over to me and said, "I am glad that Uncle John isn't paying for this."

Franco's father also came by our table and brought us a bottle of the same wine.

"I see the boys have already beaten me to it. Anyway, Dr. Weissman, I'm leaving the bottle. Enjoy, free of charge to you. Franco keeps telling Mama that he wants to return to Guyana soon. He claims he likes the weather there but now I believe it is the girls. Look at this beautiful lady you have with you. Franco says she is from Guyana. He spent a lot of time at her house when he was there. If you don't mind, Dr. Weissman, I'll return later and take this lovely lady over to meet Mama."

After he left, John came over and said, "I have been watching this table, what's with all the excitement and special treatment? Even the owner seems to be serving you, David. Why?"

"It's not me, Uncle John. It's Arshana. She has been given two bottles of wine, and as you know, she doesn't even drink."

John took up one of the bottles of wine, read the label, and said, "Do you know how expensive this wine is?"

"I just told Mom that I'm glad you aren't paying."

"Pour me a glass, David. I might never have the opportunity again."

David poured John a glass. He then poured a glass for me, and one for himself. Then he passed the bottle to Ramona and Brian.

"Arshana, do you know those boys?" John asked, looking at Vish and Franco.

"One of them is related to me. The other is Franco Jr. They are in medical school in Montréal. They visited Guyana during the summer holidays and are planning to return for Christmas. I'm hoping to be there at the same time."

John said, "I'm standing in the way. The young man behind me is waiting to take your order for dinner."

After Franco brought us our dinner, he went to his mother's table and brought Arshana a dish of chicken cacciatore. He said to me, "Try a little. They call it stewed chicken in Guyana."

"I ate it every day in Guyana, Franco," I said.

"You were in Guyana?"

"I sure was. And guess who drove us around?"

"Was it Uncle Ram? I don't believe it!"

"It certainly was. And he mentioned you and Vish all the time."

"Uncle Ram is one of the nicest guys I've ever met," Franco said. "He drove us from the East Coast to the West Coast off Demerara and because we were students, he refused to take a single penny from us. Every so often we would go to his house for lunch. His wife makes the best fish curry in the world. I told my mama, the only way I like to eat fish is when it is cooked in curry. And she would always reply, 'If you want to eat fish curry, Franco, marry a Guyanese girl.

"Oh, I have to return to my table," he said. "The band is getting ready to start and my customers are still waiting for dessert."

Vish took our orders for dessert and coffee and brought Arshana a huge dish of ice cream. "For you," he said. "I know you can put this away in no time. You love ice cream."

To the rest of us, Vish explained, "When we were kids, we got to-gether every Saturday night and made ice cream. We took turns churn-ing it by hand on a wooden ice cream maker, and Arshana always got the biggest share. She was the youngest and every one favoured her."

"Vish, stop giving my secrets away," said Arshana. "Now go and finish your work. People are on the dance floor."

Vish left just as John came back to our table.

"How was dinner?" John asked.

Everyone agreed that it was excellent.

And to David he said, "I don't believe you know Simon Goodwin. He is one of our senior partners. I'd like you to meet him."

As soon as John and David left, Martha and Sarah walked over to our table. "We're going to the ladies," Sarah said, "anyone care to join us? How about you Ruth? You seem to be having a good time."

"Of course I am," I replied. "And I really don't feel like getting up and walking all the way to the ladies room. I'm okay for now, thank you."

"Ramona, don't you want to go to the ladies?" Sarah asked.

"I've been already," Ramona replied.

Pointing to the empty wine bottles on the table, Sarah said, "I hope your father isn't paying the bill for all of that."

"I can assure you Mom, Dad isn't paying," said Ramona. As Martha and Sarah were leaving, Martha said to Sarah, "It pays to know the right people, especially the waiters. We're moving with the wrong crowd."

"Martha," I said, "you aren't happy unless you're insulting people. Just go to the washroom and leave us alone."

After they walked away, Eric, who was sitting opposite us, got up and came and stood behind my chair.

"Auntie Ruth," he said to me, "you are all having a good time and we're getting ignored at our end of the table."

"That isn't true, Eric," I said. "Why do you think that you are being ignored? Aren't you having a good time?"

"I would have a better time if this young lady would smile at me." He leaned over my chair, placed one arm on my shoulder and the other on Arshana's.

Arshana almost shuddered and his hand slipped off.

"Eric, take your hand off immediately and go and sit with the beautiful young woman who came with you," I said.

"I didn't bring anyone, that's Cynthia's friend. They work together."

When he didn't get a reply, he seemed to get desperate.

"Auntie Ruth," he continued, "Listen, the music has just begun. Can you persuade this young lady to dance with me?" He then tried to pull Arshana off her chair.

Arshana said quietly but firmly, "Don't touch me, please."

"Who the hell do you think you are?" Eric was getting belligerent.

"You might be wearing a $2000 designer dress but you can't hide the fact that you are still a maid."

"Leave her alone," Brian stood up. "You are making a scene."

"Do you think you're better than me?" asked Eric.

"At least I'm not a coward," Brian said. "You waited until David was not at the table and then you came over here to be a nuisance."

"If I were you, Brian, I would keep quiet," Eric said, "I know all about you. You and the lady are gold diggers. You married Ramona for her money, and this little schemer is trying to scam David."

"That's enough," Ramona said. "Get back to your seat. Of all days, do not make a scene today. Dad will never forgive you. You can barely stand up."

"I'm probably drunk because I was drinking cheap liquor; the expensive stuff was served to people like you for free."

David was still talking with John and Simon Goodwin, but his eyes were on our table. He excused himself and came over to our table. He was mad. Very mad.

"What the hell is going on?" he ground out. "For God's sake Eric, are you going to ruin every party. Tonight is not the night. Have you no respect for your father and his firm and guests?"

Carl, who was spied his drunk son, walked over to the table and said to Eric in a voice like ice, "Get back to your seat at once." Without a word, Eric obeyed.

"And Arshana," he said, "I'm so sorry about all of this."

"It's not your fault, Carl," I said. "We've had a good time and Arshana was happy to run into her friends from Guyana. And if you don't mind, please tell John we are leaving now."

Franco Senior saw us standing and realized that we were about to leave, so he came over to us and asked David if the food and service was satisfactory.

"It was excellent," David said.

"Are you planning to leave now?" asked Franco. "You can't, Dr. Weissman. Mama would kill me. You don't want to see me dead. I promised her that I would take this young lady over to meet her."

And to John, who had come to our table to say goodbye, he asked, "Was everything to your satisfaction tonight, Johnny?"

"Everything was great, Franco," John said. "And now, I'll treat you and the doctor to a very good liqueur."

"Franco," Franco Sr. gestured to his son, "bring me a bottle of liqueur from mama's table."

Franco Jr. returned with the liqueur almost immediately.

"Bring some glasses, Franco," Franco Sr. said.

I was more interested in the bottle than the liqueur it contained. It was one of the most beautiful bottles that I had ever seen. It was shaped like a flying angel.

"Now, Dr. Weissman, you and Johnny enjoy. You will love this liqueur. And now I'm taking this young lady over to meet Mama," said Franco Sr.

Arshana got up, but hesitated. She looked towards me for approval and when she saw me smiling, she went along with Franco.

Later, as I glanced over to Mama's table, I saw Arshana laughing. It seemed as though she was having a good time and not very long afterwards, she was on the dance floor with one of Mama's guests. I learned later that he was one of Mama's nephews. He was dressed in a custom-tailored Italian suit and looked so confident as he whirled Arshana around the dance floor.

At one point he tightened his arm around her, drew her closer to him, and whispered something in her ear. Arshana tilted her head back and laughed. It looked as if the evening had become pleasant again for Arshana.

David was looking at her the whole time. I knew him very well and from the look in his eyes, I was certain that he was not pleased.

Following the dance, the young man with whom Arshana was dancing brought her back to our table. He then bowed, kissed her hand, thanked her for the dance and walked away.

It only took a few minutes for Arshana to look uncomfortable with the way Eric was staring at her again. In order to avoid any further trouble, I said to David, "David I know you did not have the opportunity to dance with Arshana or anyone else, but I think it is best that we leave."

"Arshana seems to have had a good time on the dance floor," he said. He looked at her and she bowed her head.

There was definitely a hint of jealousy in his voice. I knew he cared for Arshana quite a bit and protected her at all times, so I wondered if his feelings for her had progressed beyond friendship. David and I were always honest with each other so I decided that I would have a talk with him the following day.

I said goodbye to Joanne, but refused to say anything to Sarah or Martha. I didn't want to hear any of their remarks.

"Are you leaving, Auntie Ruth?" Ramona asked. "I think we will leave also."

Vish and Franco were standing next to Mama's table and Arshana asked me if she could go and say goodbye to them.

"Certainly, I will come with you if you want me to."

As we walked towards Mama's table, she said, "I guess you are leaving."

"Yes," Arshana said.

"The boys are leaving very early in the morning. I don't know when they're coming back, but when they do, please ask them to bring you over to my house to visit me," said Mama.

She then took up the beautiful centerpiece from the table and gave it to Arshana. It was a Swarovski crystal ball in which the flowers were masterfully displayed. It must have been a one-of-a-kind.

"Franco, Franco?" called Mama.

"Here, Mama."

"When you were in Guyana, you ate every day at this lady's house and I know you, Franco, you eat like a horse. You must pay something back. Now go to the kitchen and pack some meat and cheese for her to take home."

"Yes, Mama."

Franco Sr. was two tables away, talking with other customers.

He waved at David, "See you next week, Dr. Weissman."

As we were about to walk out of the restaurant, John came walking hurriedly towards us.

"Ruth, just wait a minute. I hope that incident with that idiot Eric did not prevent you from enjoying yourself."

And to Arshana he said, "Sorry, little lady. Of all days I thought he would behave himself today. We will have to stop inviting him."

"Auntie Martha and Uncle Carl would get Eric help, if they could accept the fact that there's something wrong with him in the first place," Ramona said.

"When they do realize, it will be too late," said David.

"Shana, Shana, wait a minute," Franco came running towards us with a bag in his hand. Vish followed close behind him.

Franco gave the bag to Arshana, "This is for you."

"We can't stay," said Vish. "We have to get back to our tables."

Both boys then hugged and kissed Arshana and promised that if they didn't see her again before she went back to Guyana, they would come and visit her there.

Tears were in Arshana's eyes but she walked away hoping that no one would notice.

"There's the valet with your car," she said to David. She was still carrying the flowers, so she passed them over to me, to get a better grip on the bag. She opened the bag, looked inside and pulled out a bottle of wine.

"This is for you, Uncle John," she said, handing him the bottle. "I know you will get into a lot of trouble for inviting such a disruptive guest."

John hugged her as he took the bottle and said, "Don't worry about me, little girl. It's been a long time now that I have known to turn a deaf ear to gossip."

Ramona, who was standing close by, said, "We see that bottle, Dad. It isn't fair for you to get that, I'm keeping it."

"Oh no you're not," John said.

He handed the bottle back to Arshana and said, "I can't walk back into the restaurant with this bottle. Take it home and put it somewhere safe for me. Don't let David get his hands on it. I'll be over sometime this week to collect it. I must go now. I have to write a cheque for Franco. So bye everyone, I'll see you all soon."

16

Snow fell heavily all night long and when I woke up the next morning and peeked through my bedroom window, I saw that my entire garden was covered with a blanket of snow. I pushed open my window as far as I possibly could and inhaled some of that cool fresh air. I felt so refreshed. Afterwards, I slipped on my robe, went to the bathroom, brushed my teeth, passed a comb quickly through my hair and headed for the kitchen.

There was fresh brewed coffee in the percolator. The table was set for breakfast, but there was no sign of anyone.

David probably heard me shuffling around in the kitchen and called out, "Is that you, Mom? I'm in the living room."

He was standing by the window looking down at Arshana and René. René was trying his best to get the snow blower started and Arshana was either helping him or getting in his way. It was hard to tell which was true.

"Look at her," I said. "No scarf or gloves and her coat isn't even buttoned up."

David tapped on the window and they both looked up.

"I'll be up in a minute," Arshana called out. She looked like a kid in wonderland, cupping the snow in her hands and burying her face in it. René was watching like a proud papa as if he had created the snow that so delighted her.

A few minutes later, she and René joined us in the kitchen.

"I'm sorry, Mom. I didn't know you were up," she was breathless from running up the stairs.

"You better walk carefully," said David.

"I have spoken to her many times, Dr. David, but she doesn't listen. She always seems to be in a hurry," René said. "Not good in winter."

"She is enjoying her first winter in Canada," David said. Arshana was not only huffing and puffing but shivering.

David poured her and René a cup of coffee.

"This is the first time I have seen snow," Arshana said. "Let me go out and enjoy it. After breakfast, I'll go down again and help René."

"No thanks, Miss Arshana. You will help me more by staying upstairs. I know now what the problem is and I will get the blower running in no time," said René.

"So are we having eggs for breakfast?" Arshana asked. She got up and was just about to open the fridge but I said to her, "Please sit down. We have bagels and cream cheese and that's what we're going to have."

The four of us sat down and ate. After breakfast, René got up and said, "I'll go and clean our driveway and when I am finished, I'll go over and do Mrs. Chopra's."

René shook his head saying, "I swear Ma'am, had it not been for Dr. Chopra, I would never have touched that driveway. That Mrs. Chopra only finds fault with my work."

"Come on, René," laughed David. "You are helping her out of the goodness of your heart."

"Dr. David," he said, "I have heard the saying that whatever goes around comes around. Every day, I try to figure out what sin I have committed and I can't come up with an answer. All I know is that there are two witches on earth and I have the pleasure of knowing both of them: My wife and Mrs. Chopra."

"You are bad, René," Arshana swatted him with the tea towel. "The things you say. Any one who didn't know you would think it was true."

Shaking his head, René said, "I'll go and do my work now."

After René left, Arshana asked me, "What are we going to have for dinner?"

"Leftovers," I said. "There's so much food in the fridge."

"Alright," said Arshana. "Then after I have straightened up the kitchen, I'd like to go and visit my friends."

"You're not planning to go out in this weather, are you?" David said. "It's still snowing."

"Sita made a very important appointment for me and I have to keep it."

"If you must go," I said, "clean out the fridge and take all the food with you. We'll never eat it all and there's no reason for it to end up in the garbage."

"Thank you, Mom."

"Arshana," I said to her, "this is November and if you're planning to stay in Canada after your visa expires in January, you'll have to apply for an extension now. Uncle John has promised to help you and if you feel too shy to ask him, I have a friend here in Mississauga who is a law-yer and I'm sure he would be willing to help you."

"Mom, I am still going to do this the right away by applying at the Canadian embassy," Arshana said. "Sone people who visited Sita were picked up a couple of weeks ago and deported."

"But that was due to all the illegal activities they were involved in," David said.

"My main concern is to return to Guyana to see my grandmother."

"Mom, you can't convince her," David said. "Arshana does exactly what she pleases. For instance, on a day like today, she has no right to go out. The streets are slippery with ice."

"But I'm not walking on the streets," she said. "I am going through the fields. I have a very important appointment which I must keep."

Before anything else was said, the phone rang and she answered it and handed it to me, "It's Sarah."

"Ruth," said Sarah, "it is almost impossible to get in touch with you these days and now that I managed to get you, I am going to extend Joanne's invitation to you. She has complimentary tickets for the Falls View casino in Niagara Falls this coming weekend. Meals, rooms, al-most everything is included. She wants you to join us."

"Oh, how nice of Joanne to think of me," I said. "But I already have something planned for this weekend. Let me see if I can change things around and I'll get back to you tomorrow."

"Ruth," Sarah continued, "only last night, Martha and I were say-ing that since you've had that bloody girl staying at your house, things haven't been the same. When we invite you out, you always make some excuse not to come, and you no longer invite us over. We're warning you that if you don't take our advice and get rid of that girl, you'll be very sorry. Haven't you noticed the way David looks at her? Open your eyes, she's out to get him, and take my word, she will."

David was sitting in silence. His facial muscles tensed.

"Arshana," he said, "you don't listen. You are so stubborn. Let us help you get an extension before it is too late."

She made no reply. She just walked away.

David and I walked back into the living room and watched René. He had cleaned most of the driveway. Five minutes later, Arshana joined us in the living room. She was dressed and ready to leave. One of my silk scarves was lying on a chair in the living room.

"Put that scarf around your neck," I said to her.

She picked up the scarf, wrapped it around her neck and said, "It feels so soft and warm."

"René's car is parked on the road. Why don't you let him drive you?" David suggested.

"What for? It'll only take me 15 minutes to run through the fields."

"But it isn't summer, Arshana," I said. "There is plenty of snow on the ground and you can fall and hurt yourself."

"I'll be very careful, Mom. I want to enjoy walking in the snow."

Before David and I could say anything else, she quickly picked up two bags which contained the food she was taking to her friends and fled out the door.

David and I stood by the window and watched her as she crossed the road and plowed her way through the snow. Twice she rested the bags with the food on the snow-covered ground, turned around and waved at us. She was not wearing a hat and her long hair blew in the wind.

"Mom, have you ever met any of her friends?" David asked.

"No, Arshana does not want her friends to know who we are. They don't even know that she lives just across the field from them. She told them that she was working as a nanny in Burlington and that she gets the chance to visit them when her employer goes shopping in the nearby mall. She often told me that the people Sita and Rita hang around with are not very nice people."

"But why does she go there?" David asked.

"She said it was the only way to keep in touch with Guyana. Once

I suggested that she try and break off her ties with them, and you know what her reply was? 'Mom, if push comes to shove, they will stand up for me. I'm not so sure that you would.'"

I worried about Arshana, and hoped she was safe outside. I must have got lost in my thoughts, because the next thing I knew, René was calling to me.

"Ma'am, Ma'am, where are you?"

"In the living room, René."

"Ma'am, Miss Arshana left more than an hour ago. She should have returned by now. I'll give her another half an hour and if she does not show up, I'll go and drive around the area where I believe her friends live. It is getting dark early these days and the ravine at the bottom of the field is very steep. It would be easy for her to fall and hurt herself."

David went to his room and returned a few minutes later with a book. He sat by the window and kept turning the pages, but I knew he was not concentrating. He had a blank expression and every so often he would glance at his watch and look through the window. I sat and watched quietly for a while, and then I said to him, "David you and I have always had a good mother-son relationship. We have never hidden anything from each other so I'm going to ask you this question point-blank: Are you in love with Arshana?"

He was silent for a while and then he said, "The very first time I laid eyes on her, something drew me to her. I had just returned from Bermuda and she was cooking something. I said hi to her, but she never replied. She barely lifted her head and smiled.

"As the days went by, I found myself eager to come home from work and see her. She was always there waiting to serve me dinner with a smile. She spoke very little and since she was a guest in our house, I avoided any contact with her. I stayed overnight with friends and couldn't wait to get home to see her. I fell head over heels in love with her and then one evening, you went over to Auntie Sarah's to play cards. I was sitting in this very chair and she came and asked me whether she could get me something to eat.

"I told her no, and she said she was just running out to make a phone call and she would be back shortly. When I suggested to her to use the phone in the house, she said that she didn't want anyone to know the phone number. I sat and watched as she ran through the fields, and half an hour later, she returned and went straight to her room. I was sitting by the window and she never said a word to me. I felt that there was something wrong, so I went and knocked on her door.

"When she opened her door, I saw that her hair was all disheveled, her dress was torn and there was blood all over! 'What happened?' I asked, 'Were you attacked on your way home? I'll call the police?' But she begged me not to. 'Then you better tell me what happened or I will have to call the police.' She was shaking and sobbing and I said, 'Arshana I'm going to ask you one more time. What happened?'

"And she finally told me. When she went over to Sita's, she saw a man there who didn't look like the usual drug addicts. He was nicely dressed and appeared to be very polite. He wasn't. He grabbed her and asked Sita if Arshana was a working girl. Sita said that Arshana was not the type, but this man, George, he told Sita that she was crazy. He said 'With a beautiful girl like this, we can make tons of money. We're sitting on a gold mine.' He said he knew a few big clients who would pay top dollar for her. In fact, he told Arshana that he was one of the richest and most powerful men in Mississauga. He groped Arshana and she screamed. Sita told George to leave her alone. But George was so persistent, he began tearing Arshana's clothes off and when Sita saw that he wouldn't stop, she grabbed a vase and hit him on the head. George began to bleed, and that gave Arshana a chance to run away.

"I told her to take a shower and find some clean clothes. Then I went to the kitchen and made her some tea with a mild sedative to help her sleep.

"'Please don't tell Mom what happened to me tonight,' she begged me. I told her I would think about it. She said that because she was a maid, people might think that she doesn't deserve respect. I told her I respected her.

"Then I walked towards the door and when I turned around, I saw her sitting on the bed with her legs curled up under her chin and she was crying. 'Please don't leave me right now,' she begged, 'I need someone to be with me. I need my grandmother.'

"'I can't help you there,' I had said, but I offered to sit with her for a while, and she let me. I sat on the bed with her and put my arms around her. For a while I sat motionless with thoughts in turmoil. She lifted her face close to mine, put her arms around me and said, 'This isn't something a well brought up girl would do but I am asking you not to leave me tonight. I can't bear to stay by myself.'

"I stayed with her that night, and every time there was an opportunity, I went to her room and spent the night with her. I fell hopelessly and helplessly in love with her. Night and other women meant nothing to me anymore. I just looked forward to coming home and spending the evening with her.

"She would stand at the door and welcome me with a lovely smile. Of course, there was always a delicious home-cooked meal waiting for me. For some reason I had a gut feeling that I would come home one day to find her gone. That thought always bothered me.

"Then I fell sick, but she took care of me, giving up many nights of sleep to attend to me. It was the very first time in my life where I felt really close to someone who wasn't you or Dad, and as the days passed by, I fell more and more in love with her. I couldn't imagine spending the rest of my life without her, so I asked her to marry me.

"'You are still delirious from your fever,' she had said to me, 'Do you know the ridicule you and your mother would face if you married me? Not to mention the consequences!' I asked her what consequences she could possibly be referring to, and reminded her that I don't have to answer to anyone when I make life decisions.

"'Arshana, are you trying to avoid my proposal of marriage?' I had asked, 'Because if you are involved with anyone in Guyana, let me know. If you are, I promise you that I will stay away from you and never bring up this matter again.'

"She told me that she wasn't, and that the only person she cared about was her grandmother. She said that she didn't want to hurt her, and I said that if that was the case, we could start working on her visa right away. I offered the help of my lawyer friends, I told her we could get married and she could come with me on my trip to India. I remembered how often she would say that her ancestors came from India.

"But she said, 'David, why don't we leave things as they are right now? You go to India and I will go to Guyana and I will return as soon as I can. If you still want to marry me, we can do it then.'

"I asked her if that's what she wanted, and she said, 'No, it's not what I want but I think it would be better this way. David, you have made me so happy by asking me to marry you.'

"I had the feeling that she was about to leave at any moment, so I kept on bugging her to marry me, but she would always smile and say, 'David let's enjoy today.'"

Getting to the end of his story, David said "Mom, now that you know that I'm in love with her, I'm going to do whatever it takes to get her to marry me, maybe as soon as next week."

"As you wish, David," I said. "Whatever makes you happy makes me happy. We just have to hope that René's fears don't come true and he brings Arshana home soon." I got up, left him still sitting by the window and went to my room.

17

I woke up feeling very hungry and then it dawned on me that I had eaten very little the day before. I got dressed and went down to the kitchen to make myself breakfast. David had made a pot of coffee before he left for work, so I poured myself a cup. I popped a couple of slices of bread into the toaster but after buttering them, I no longer felt hungry. Arshana had been missing for four days. I was sick with worry.

I heard the snow blower going at full blast beneath my window and I knew that René was clearing the driveway.

I tapped on the window and yelled out to him. He looked up and when he saw me he turned off the blower and came walking slowly up the stairs

"Good morning Ma'am," he looked sad.

"You are worried about Arshana, aren't you, René?"

"Ma'am, we have not heard a single word from her in four days. This isn't like her. Something is terribly wrong Ma'am. I can feel it."

"I don't know what we can do, René," I said. "Let's have some coffee and I will go and drive around the area where her friends live."

"It's not easy driving on that street. I don't believe they have cleaned it since the first snowfall and cars are parked all over the place."

"Her friends live about 15 minutes from here, isn't that right, René?"

"Could be even less, depending on the traffic. When you get to the bottom of the street, turn right and then right again at the very first traffic light. Soon afterwards, maybe a minute away, you will see a row of townhouses. I believe her friends live in one of those houses. Ma'am, the streets are slippery and it is still foggy outside. Why don't you wait until after lunch? The skies will clear and the sun will come out."

"Look René, look towards the sky."

A single ray of sunshine was peeping through the clouds.

"It's a good sign, René. I'll get my coat and boots." As René walked me to my car, he insisted that he should accompany me.

"No René, let me go alone. Let me try my luck."

The road was very slippery but I drove slowly. As René had said, it barely took me 15 minutes to track down the townhouses.

The townhouses were exactly alike. I kept asking myself 'Which one? Which one?' I drove up and down the street, stopping occasionally to check out the townhouses. And then out of the blue, a man came walking out of one of the houses. He walked towards his car which was covered with snow, took out a scraper from the trunk and began to clean the snow from his car.

I drove slowly towards him and as I got closer, his features reminded me so much of Ram, the taxi driver that I met in Guyana. I got out of my car and said to him, "Excuse me, sir, seeing that you live around here, I was wondering if you could help me. I was told that some young ladies lived in the area and I thought perhaps you might know them. I believe one of them is called Sita," Arshana had often mentioned her name.

"Ladies? Ladies?!" He looked me over from head to toe and said, "You look like a pretty decent lady to me. I can't see why you would want to get in touch with them. My guess is that they ripped you off too." Pointing to one of the houses he said, "They all live there. Sita is the head bitch."

"What do you know about them?" I asked.

"Ma'am," he said, "I don't know why you are looking for those criminals, but I am advising you not to set foot in that house."

When he saw that I wasn't going to give up, he shrugged and said, "Good luck, lady. I have to go and open my store, I'm already late."

Then he got into his car and drove away. When he had left, I walked back to my car and sat there for a while. After I felt that I had built up enough courage, I got out of the car and walked slowly towards the house. Knowing about the character of the occupants, I was nervous. To be cautious, I stopped and looked around and listened before I climbed the stairs.

I stood in front of the door for a few minutes before I knocked.

There was no answer, so I waited for a moment, then rapped again.

"Who's there? Come in," I heard a voice say. The door was unlocked and when I pushed it open, there was a young woman sitting on the couch.

As soon as she saw me, she jumped up and said, "Who the hell are you?"

I was scared. My legs were shaking, but I didn't want her to know that.

"I'll get straight to the point," I said. "I am looking for Arshana. A few days ago she left to come here and I have not seen nor heard from her since. She had an important appointment which she never went to, so I would appreciate any information you could give me about her."

"I don't know anyone by that name," said the girl, who I assumed had to be Sita.

"Oh yes you do," I pointed to the silk scarf that I had given Arshana to wear the day she left home.

"You can pick up a scarf like that anywhere in Mississauga. I bought it at one of the flea markets," the girl said.

"Not like that one, I bought that scarf a few years ago in Japan. Look Sita, all I am asking you is to tell me where Arshana is. Did George or one of your millionaire clients hurt her? She said you protected her and hit George on the head with a vase. You're lucky that Arshana didn't want to call the police. She didn't want to get anyone in trouble."

I had been standing since I entered the house, so I asked her if I could sit down for a minute. She pointed to a chair and as I was about to sit, another young woman came out of the bedroom.

"You must be Rita," I said.

"How the hell do you know our names?" Sita asked.

"Are you from immigration or the police?" asked Rita.

"Neither. I am a close friend of Arshana's. She has mentioned your names. She said you were all very close friends in Guyana. I always give her food to bring for you all. I was helping her to get her visa extended, so it bothered me when she missed her appointment with the lawyer."

I opened my purse and took out two hundred dollar bills. I knew the sight of money would make them talk. And it did, their eyes lit up. "I'll give you $100 each for some information about Arshana."

"Okay lady, I should not tell you this, but Arshana came here last week and asked Sita to make arrangements for her to have an abortion."

"Was she pregnant?"

"Of course she is," Sita said angrily. "If she wasn't pregnant, why would she need an abortion?"

"It's just that I'm shocked. She knows me very well and she never mentioned being pregnant."

"We know a couple of nurses who work in one of the hospitals around here," said Rita. "They do abortions under the table to finance their drug habit. Their fee is $400 for an abortion, which is cheaper than the clinics. Arshana paid them the $400, but they didn't do the operation, nor did they return the money. We're going to get that money back for Arshana sooner or later."

Sita said, "It wasn't altogether their fault. Arshana could not tell them how many months pregnant she was. As they were about to perform the operation, Arshana screamed and fainted. It scared the hell out of all of us and the male nurse told me this was too much trouble for him, he wasn't going to do the operation in case there were complications and Arshana tried to go to the police."

Rita said, "It took a while for Arshana to recover after she had fainted. The female nurse suggested that we drive her to the hospital to make sure her elevated stress levels weren't dangerous. I told her that Arshana had no OHIP benefits, but she said she would be on duty in about an hour to take care of her. Rita and I did as she told us. That was the last time we saw Arshana."

"No one wants to know where Arshana is more than I do," said Sita. "I brought her into this country and will never have peace of mind till I find out what has happened to her. So please, lady, I'm begging you, please let us deal with this by ourselves. Yesterday we gave the two nurses a few more days to come up with some information and if they don't, some of our friends will be paying them a visit. They will return Arshana and her money to us. Trust me, they will be in touch."

"So lady," said Rita, "Return to your church or whatever and let us handle the situation. If we hear from Arshana, we will let her know that you came looking for her."

Sita then walked me to the door and closed it with a loud bang. I walked slowly down the stairs with my knees shaking. When I got to my car, I sat for a few minutes to compose myself before I drove off. My mind was in turmoil. I took my time driving slowly towards home, not because of the slippery road, but because I could not stop crying. My eyes were blurry and every nerve in my body was twitching. When I finally reached home, I was barely able to haul my body up the stairs. I sat on the first available chair when I entered the house, leaned back and closed my eyes.

I didn't realize that David was home until he joined me in the living room.

"Are you all right, Mom?" he asked.

"I was over at Sita's place and I'm not so happy with the information I got from her. They have no idea where Arshana is, whether she's dead or alive."

"What does that mean?"

"Arshana was pregnant and asked Sita to arrange an abortion for her. Something went wrong and no one knows what happened to Arshana after she entered the hospital."

He squeezed his eyes shut and sat down.

He said "Why didn't she talk to me? Why didn't she come to me for help? She was having my child. If I had only known that she was pregnant, I finally could have convinced her to marry me. She would have listened to me eventually.

"How could I have been so stupid? What kind of doctor am I? Every day, dozens of people come to the office demanding to see Dr. Weissman. 'Dr. Weissman is one of the best doctors. He can work miracles.' Where was Dr. Weissman when the only woman he ever loved needed him?"

Then David asked with a pained look in his eyes, "Did she have the abortion?"

"No one knows, David. She would have had to go to one of the hospitals around here."

"I can find out," he said. "Oh my God, I thought she had left me. Left us. That I had scared her away."

"David, are you out of your mind? Arshana did everything she could to protect us. If you go poking around and someone finds out that Arshana has had an abortion and died, just think of who people are going to blame.

"You. They will blame you, David. Sita and Rita will try to save their own skin and they will swear that Arshana told them that you did the abortion. Just think of the headlines. 'Wealthy doctor kills maid because she was pregnant by him.' So David, as your mother, I am begging you to leave everything in the hands of Sita and Rita. Remember, Arshana protected us to the very end. No one knows about our connection to her," I pleaded with him. "If Arshana is alive, she will get in touch with us, but if she's dead there's nothing we can do."

"I can never have peace until I know what has happened to her," David said. Then he walked to Arshana's room, and eventually retreated into his own room.

David hadn't been eating, René was as sad as I had ever seen him, and I didn't know what to do with myself. I was glad when I heard the doorbell, because it finally gave me a distraction from my worry. When I opened the door, I saw Dr. Taylor standing there.

"Sorry to barge in on you like this, Ruth; I meant to phone you before I left from the lawyer's office but it completely slipped my mind. I hope this is a convenient time."

"Why, any time is convenient, Dr. Taylor," I said, trying to smile.

David got up from the couch on which he was lying and said, "Have a seat, sir. I'm sorry you found me unshaven and still in my pajamas."

"I'm glad I did, David, or I would've thought that you were playing hooky and avoiding work. You really do look sick, lad," Dr. Taylor said. "Stay home for another week and get all the rest you can. Remember our trip to India isn't too far off and I want you to be good and healthy before we leave."

Dr. Taylor continued, "Of late I have not been feeling well, so today I went to my lawyer's office to make sure that he had drawn up my will exactly as I told him to. For years I have been telling you that whatever I have accumulated in this lifetime will be yours when I leave this world. Today I signed my will, leaving everything to you, with only two requests.

"My first request is that you take good care of my Becky. My will ensures that my wife will have all the worldly possessions she needs once I'm gone, but money can't keep her safe and happy; that's up to you. My second request is that you visit and look after my leprosy hospital in India whenever possible.

"As you know, my father spent his life working as a missionary doctor in India. He did not believe in preaching but in helping the sick and poor. Most of his work was done in the rural areas among the lepers. Before he died, he built the leprosy hospital. Over the years I have made it much bigger and people are coming from all over India to be treated.

"There's a group of people who are very dedicated and involved with the hospital. I know most of them personally and I am sure they will give you all the help you may need in the years to come.

"I'm sure you are aware of the terrible stigma surrounding leprosy, not only in India, but all over the world. But we both know that leprosy is curable if caught early, and though I won't live to see it, I can imagine a world in which the disease is completely eradicated. I am going to tell you what my father told me in my final year of medical school: Remember that true humility is serving all of humanity and loving your fellow human beings.

"Think of the poor and those affected with awful diseases. The rich may pay you well, but they will forget you in a minute. The poor have nothing, but they will always remember what you've done for them.

"I promised my dad that I would continue to look after his hospital as long as I could. Over the years, I have tried my best. You have seen me travel to India twice or three times a year but I feel that this is my last trip. That is the main reason I want you to go with me, with the hope that you would continue this work for me.

"David, you were born with that precious gift of knowing exactly what to say to people.

"I hate to admit this, but since your office is right beside mine, sometimes when your doors are open, I sit and eavesdrop and laugh my head off. I'm always so amazed by how you soothe and flatter those old cronies. And if I may say, you do a pretty good job with the young ones too.

"David, I don't think I have ever come right out and told you how I feel about you, but you know in your heart my feelings towards you. You are loved and respected by all the doctors in our office. I'm not only referring to the female ones, but everyone.

"Yesterday I was so pleased with the reaction I received from some of the doctors when I told them of my decision to turn over the office to you. I gave them two options. They could stay or sell their practice, and unanimously they agreed to stay on and work with you.

"I was in this business before you were born David, and I have never seen such loyalty and friendship among doctors. And when you do take over, put Nancy Fine in charge of the office and the staff.

"David, I hope I'm not burdening you with too much responsibility, you are still so very young."

"I'll give it my best shot, sir," David said.

Dr. Taylor said, "My father told me that when the burden became too great for me, I should hand it over to my son. But since the good Lord has not blessed Becky and me with children, the only person I feel can take the place of a son is you. A couple of nights ago, I was very restless in bed. I kept twisting and turning. Becky got up, turned the lights on and said, 'Out with it, Don. Something is bothering you. What is it?' I asked her, 'Becky, who should I leave to look up on you and tend to your needs when I'm gone?'

"'You aren't going anywhere for a long time, Don,' she said, 'but if the good Lord decides to take you before me, leave David to look after me. I don't want any of your relatives or my relatives to do the job. We only see or hear from them if they need something.'

"I think my wife was right. David, now that I have passed everything over to you, it is my wish that someday you will pass whatever you acquire on to your son."

David bent his head, and placed both hands on his forehead.

"Are you alright, David?" Dr. Taylor asked. "For a moment you looked so white, I thought you were going to pass out."

"He has barely eaten anything for the past few days," I said.

"Maybe a good shot of brandy will cheer him up. I can do with one myself," Dr. Taylor said.

David got up and poured a brandy for me, Dr. Taylor and for himself.

As Dr. Taylor sipped his brandy, he said, "David, don't believe everything you hear about the dirt and poverty in India. A lot of it is true, but you will find that India is one of the most fascinating countries in the world. You'll hate it at first but as time goes by, you'll learn to love it. Becky hates when I say it, but believe me, India has some of the most beautiful woman in the world. And now, I'll have another quick brandy, Becky is sure to have my supper waiting for me and when I'm late she gives me hell.

"Take my advice David, when you find a wife, make sure you find one who will stay home, cook your meals and wait for you at the door when you come home from work."

And as he was about to leave, he tapped David on his shoulder, and said "Take a few more days off. Get all the rest you can. I'll see you next week."

David then walked him to the door and said goodbye to him.

18

A few days had passed and David and I were trying to decide whether we ought to go to Cynthia's party when the phone rang.

It was Cynthia. "Auntie Ruth," she said, "I was just calling everyone to remind them to be at the restaurant no later than six o'clock. I have arranged for dinner to be served at seven. So there will be plenty of time to have a couple of drinks before dinner."

"Cynthia, David is still fighting this terrible flu. Look, he is right here, speak to him," I said.

David took the phone. I couldn't hear what Cynthia was saying to him but I heard David say, "If you want me to come and spread my germs around I'll try to be there, at least for a short while."

After he hung up the phone, he said, "If we have to be there for six we have to start getting dressed now. It is almost five o'clock."

After I got dressed and came downstairs, he was already dressed and standing before Arshana's door. He was wearing the same suit and tie he wore when he took Arshana and me to dinner at the same restaurant we were going to tonight.

"Mom, I was just remembering how Arshana was so scared when I asked her to dance."

"How could I forget? I had to nudge her several times under the table before she would get up."

"I can't get her out of my mind. I keep thinking of every little thing she did or said." He was silent for a moment, then he said, "Want to go now? We're only 15 minutes from the restaurant. We would probably be early."

But we were not early. In fact, we were late. Everyone was there.

"I thought you weren't coming," Cynthia said as she led us to our table. "I placed you with the older folks and David with the younger ones," she told me.

"You look 40 or 50 today, Cynthia," David asked jokingly.

"Count your blessings that you do look sick, David, or I would have jumped on you."

Martha heard them and said, "The only way that you two are going to stop fighting is to get married."

"If we get married, Auntie Martha," David said, "we will kill each other in less than a week."

"Order something to drink," Cynthia said to David. "The waiter is standing behind you."

"Let me sit first," David replied.

We were barely seated when I saw an elderly woman approaching David's table. She looked as though she had had plenty to drink already.

"There you are, Dr. Weissman. I can spot my handsome doctor a mile away. For over three weeks I have been trying to get an appointment to see you and every time I called, I was told that you were sick with the flu. So I went over to your office and told the receptionist, 'Dr. Weissman got rid of my flu in a week. Why is it taking him so long to get rid of his flu?'

"Then she said that she wasn't a doctor so I told her that she should not be working in a medical office but in a burlesque club. I told her the next time I visited the office, I wanted to see her properly dressed. And I suggested she wear a blouse that buttons up to the neck, and is not see-through.

"She told me, 'Mrs. Johnston, if there is an emergency, I can give you an appointment with another doctor.' But I told her that I didn't want to see that elephant Dr. Fine or that old bag Dr. Taylor, I wanted to see Dr. Weissman. I said, 'If I have to wait until doomsday, I will wait.'"

"I promise you, Mrs. Johnston," David said, "when I return to work, you will be the first person that will have an appointment. By the way, Mrs. Johnson have you done your hair today? I bet the dress you're wearing is new. You look so pretty tonight. Took me a while to recognize you."

"You adorable hunk, Dr. Weissman," she laughed. "You know how to flatter the ladies."

"Careful, Mrs. Johnston, you are spilling your drink. You don't want to ruin your pretty dress."

He then got up, took the glass from her, put his arm around her and said, "Now show me your table."

She showed him where she was sitting and David walked her over. He spent a few minutes chatting with the guests at her table. When he returned, dinner was announced.

During dinner, Carl ordered several bottles of champagne and we toasted Cynthia and sang happy birthday. It was a beautiful seven-course dinner which everyone enjoyed. Afterwards there was coffee and liqueur and then the band began to play music perfect for dancing.

Several of the young people got up and began to dance, including Cynthia and David. Cynthia was so drunk, she almost fell. She was lucky that David grabbed her.

John was sitting two chairs away from me, so I asked him if he enjoyed the dinner.

"It was excellent," he replied. "But I would have preferred some curry and roti."

"How about you, David?" John asked as David finished dancing and returned to his table. "By the way, David, how could you have allowed the beautiful young woman to return to Guyana? She was so sweet and innocent. I would have thought you'd put a ring on her finger by now."

"You old fool, John," Sarah said. "She wasn't sweet nor innocent. She knew exactly how to fool men."

"Sarah," I said, "from the very beginning, both you and Martha were nasty to Arshana. She was a lovely person and it is a pity that you both misjudged her. I have to admit, I miss her terribly and wish that she would return soon. And I'll admit a secret to both of you; David asked her to marry him and she refused."

"Did I hear that right?" Sarah asked.

"I believe she has had too much to drink," Martha said.

"I agree with you, Auntie Martha," David said. And to me, he said, "Mom let's go."

We made a quick exit without drawing too much attention. On our way home, David said to me, "Mom, stop defending Arshana. Let them think what they like. We both know different."

19

My room felt very stuffy, so I got out of bed, walked towards the window and opened it a few inches. A gust of fresh air blew into the room and I felt refreshed. I stood by the window inhaling all that beautiful fresh air and then went back to bed. I twisted and turned for a bit until I fell asleep.

The next morning when I woke up, I found the room very cold and realized that I had left the window open all night.

I got out of bed and went to the window to close it, but it was stuck. There was ice all around the window pane.

I tried pushing and banging on it, but the window wouldn't budge. David probably heard all the commotion and called out, "Everything all right, Mom?"

"It's my window," I shouted. "I can't get it to open or close."

David walked into the room and said, "Let me try." As soon as he touched the window, it flew open. A withered branch with a single rose on it fell through the window into the room. It brushed David's face gently.

"Oh my God," he said, "this is unbelievable. Arshana always touched my face with a rose the same way." He picked up the rose, held it close and said, "My good luck charm."

"Look David, look through the window. Look at the rosebush."

Dry, faded leaves still clung to the rosebush branches.

As Arshana had predicted, the rosebush had grown way past my window and was actually touching the roof.

"Yes, I remember the bet she made with René," David said.

He looked at his watch, "I better get my bags together; the taxi should be here any moment now."

"But David, you didn't have breakfast or even a cup of coffee."

"I got up early and made myself some coffee. I can get some food on the plane."

I followed him as he walked down the stairs. He paused for a moment in front of Arshana's room. I thought he might go into the room, but he paused briefly, closed his eyes for a moment and walked away.

"The taxi is here. The taxi is here, Dr. David," René announced as he came running up the stairs. "Let me take your bags sir," he said to David.

"Just take one of them," David told René. As he kissed me goodbye he said, "Mom you have gone through hell with me. You have suffered as much as I have, but I promise you I'll make it up to you."

"What are mothers for?" I said. "Now you go and have a good trip and I'll see you in two weeks."

I put up a brave front but as soon as he left, I broke down and cried.

I heard René coming up the stairs so I quickly wiped my tears away. René still noticed my sadness and said, "Ma'am, don't worry, two weeks will go by in no time. Remember last year when he went to that conference in China? You were so worried, and before we knew it, 17 days had passed and he was back."

I suppose I didn't look any happier, because René asked, "Ma'am, would you like me to stay around for a little while?"

"No René, thanks for asking but I'm looking forward to spending some time alone."

"I won't count on that, Ma'am, Mrs. Nadler just turned into the driveway."

I sighed. "Well, have a nice weekend, René. I'll see you on Monday morning."

"Oh no, Ma'am, I'll be here tomorrow morning. I promised the doctor that I would visit you every day until he returned. I'll now open the door for your visitors and then I will leave."

As he did so, in walked Martha, Sarah and Joanne.

"Ruth, are you still in your dressing gown?" Martha asked, "Where is David? We came early to say goodbye to him."

"He left early. He went to pick up Dr. Taylor."

"I hope our coming here will cheer you up a bit. You look sad."

"Why should I be sad?" I replied. "I am just concerned. He still hasn't completely recovered from that terrible flu."

"Where is that girl? I haven't seen her around," Sarah said.

"Are you asking about Arshana, Sarah? I wish she was here. She would have cheered me up. Both David and I have missed her so much since she left."

"Well, I for one am glad that she's gone," Martha said. "I don't care how sweet she was or what a wonderful cook she was, I hope that she has gone for good. From day one, I never trusted her. Underneath that sweet innocent face was a devil and a schemer."

"Ruth," Martha continued, "I don't suppose you noticed that she was trying to get her claws into David?"

"Everyone else did, Ruth Bunker," said Sarah.

I swear I had heard Martha and Sarah suggest that a million times, and this was the final straw. "You all got it wrong," I said. "She didn't want David, he wanted her. He asked her to marry him and she turned him down flat."

"She did what?" Sarah asked.

"You heard me. She turned him down. She refused his proposal."

"Ruth, I don't believe you. David would have to admit that to me himself. Either way, she's gone. And now, what are your plans for today?" asked Martha.

"I have no plans," I said. "And I can assure you all that I am not cooking."

"Then we will go out for lunch," Sarah said. "Let's choose a pricey restaurant. Joanne will pay. She won a huge jackpot at the Woodbine Casino yesterday."

Joanne had been sitting in silence and listening to us babbling until now. "Sarah, please don't chew my head off, but I have to agree with Ruth, the girl looked like a very nice and respectable young woman."

"Looks can be deceiving, Joanne," Sarah said. "And you ought to know."

"Now don't start on me, Sarah," Joanne said. "Let's change the subject. I'll buy lunch, but first I need a drink."

"You all know where the bar is," I said, "help yourselves. I'm going upstairs to get dressed."

When I returned 20 minutes later, Martha said, "Ruth, you better have a drink before you go. You know the price of a drink is always double in those fancy restaurants."

I joined them with a drink and we left shortly afterwards.

Two weeks later, on the day that David was getting home, I woke up to heaps of snow. I hoped David's plane hadn't been delayed because of bad weather. I knew the forecast called for even more snow, so I decided that I was not going to leave my house.

For some time, I had told myself to clean out Arshana's room and since the weather was miserable, I decided to make myself even more miserable by cleaning her room.

Arshana's room was always spotless so there wasn't much to do. Her dresses hung neatly in her closet and a few bottles were arranged on her dresser.

I felt guilty going through the room, but I wanted to clean up if Arshana was truly gone for good.

I went over to her dresser, and upon opening one of the drawers, the first thing that caught my eye was the British West Indian folder. In the folder was her passport and a return ticket to Guyana. I was convinced that she could not have left Canada.

Tears filled my eyes as I looked at her passport picture. My hands began to tremble and I sat on the bed and began to cry. I must have sat for some time, and only got up at the sound of Gladys' voice.

"Ma'am? Where are you, Ma'am?"

"In Arshana's room, Gladys."

"You have come at just the right time, Gladys. I was trying to sort out Arshana's things. I will be sending most, if not all of it, to the Salvation Army. We haven't heard a single word from her since she left, so I doubt she will come back for her stuff."

"Ma'am, if you don't mind, can I have some of her clothing?"

"Take what you like, Gladys."

"Thank you, Ma'am. I didn't get a chance to send a box home to Poland for Christmas, so I am posting one next week. I can send the clothes too." She went to the kitchen and returned with a couple of garbage bags.

As she was putting the clothes in the bags, she said to me, "Ma'am, people are coming from all over the world into Canada. And many of them claim refugee status and they are allowed to stay here. I don't know the law and I have no right to make any judgment, but I can't understand why honest and hard-working people like Miss Arshana are not permitted to stay here."

She paused looking at me. When I said nothing, she continued. "Ma'am, you could have sponsored her, couldn't you?"

"I don't think so, Gladys, she isn't my relative. She said if she decided to stay in Canada, she would go about it the right way. Also, her grandmother was quite sick and she wanted to see her, so I don't think that staying in Canada was her priority."

"I know someone is missing her terribly," said Gladys.

I thought she would have said David, but then she said, "Speaking of the devil, I just heard his voice."

"Where are you Ma'am?" called René from downstairs.

"Gladys and I are in Miss Arshana's room, René."

"Get your fat Spanish tail in here right away," Gladys yelled.

When he joined us in the room, he said to me, "Ma'am I don't believe my eyes. Is Gladys helping you? Her poor back is already damaged. You don't want to make things worse. The last time she went before the compensation board, she used a walking stick."

Gladys picked up Arshana's hairbrush, threw it at René and said, "One word from you, René, and I'll put my foot in your mouth."

"Gladys, René!" I was not in a mood for their constant bickering. "In the 20 years you both have been working for me, not a single day has gone by when you weren't at each other's throats. I am now convinced that you are in love with each other."

Both of them made retching noises.

"Ma'am, believe me, if he was the last man on earth, I wouldn't want him."

"Go, René, make us a nice pot of tea," I said. They had eased my mood.

After René left, Gladys gathered up the stuff she had selected, put it into the garbage bags and put the rest into boxes for the Salvation Army. Together we went to the kitchen and had tea and cake.

Gladys left shortly afterwards and when she was gone, René said to me, "Ma'am, it is no longer a pleasure for me to come to work. I miss Miss Arshana terribly. Many days, when you were out, I would come upstairs and she would make me a cup of coffee. We would sit at this very table and she would tell me all about Guyana. Often there were tears in her eyes. I grew to love her like my own daughter and she showed me the same respect that she would have shown her own father. There were so many times when she would come to the kitchen and cry after she had been insulted by one of your friends.

"I will never forget the night of Ms. Ramona's party. She pleaded with me to let her stay in my room until the party was over, but I told her to go and hold her head up high, but that drunk man Mr. Eric harassed her."

He got up and as he was about to leave, I looked through the window and saw that it was snowing heavily.

"René, why don't you stay in your room tonight," I suggested. "Driving home would be terrible."

"I must go, Ma'am. My wife chose today of all days to go shopping, so I have to go and pick her up."

"Well, if you must go, René, at least drive carefully. These snow trucks have been cleaning and salting the streets all day long, but there is far too much snow for them to keep up with. They will certainly have to work all night long."

"I will be over early in the morning to clean your driveway, so I will see you then, Ma'am," René said. He was about to leave when the phone rang. I told him not to answer it but he said, "Ma'am, it could be Miss Arshana."

"Alright, if it will make you happy, answer it, René," I said.

"Betty," René said, "When did you get back? I told you that boyfriend of yours was up to no good but you didn't listen to me. Yes, she is right here," he said, handing me the phone.

"Hello," I said.

"Ma'am," Betty said, "I am back and I hope my job is still open."

"As a matter-of-fact, Betty, it is."

"Thank God," Betty said. "I'll be over bright and early tomorrow morning and then we can have a long talk."

"Bye for now, Betty," I said.

When I hung up the phone, René said to me, "I'll bet you that boyfriend took all her money and disappeared."

I shook my head, "No need to gossip, René."

Just then, René's cellphone started ringing.

"Do you know who that is?" I asked.

"No," said René, looking at the number. But I could tell from the way his eyes lit up that he hoped it was Arshana.

"Hello," he said.

Whoever was on the other end of the phone was very quiet, and I couldn't hear what they were saying. All I knew was that René looked very excited.

The call ended quickly, and René said immediately, "That was Arshana!"

"Are you sure?" I asked. I couldn't believe it.

"Absolutely, I would know her voice anywhere."

He looked at his watch, "Ma'am, you said that Dr. David would be here by five. How come he isn't here yet?"

"René, I told you that his plane would land at five. He has to go through customs and stop over at Dr. Taylor's house before he gets home."

As I was speaking, David's taxi pulled up in front of the house. "I'll run down and get his bags. I can't wait to give him the news," René said.

"So good to be home," David said as he walked through the door. And before he could even sit down, René blurted out, "Sir, I heard from Miss Arshana. I believe she phoned from Guyana. I am not sure about that, but I'm certain it was her voice."

"What did she say, René?" David asked.

"Not very much, sir, but she did say she would be seeing me soon."

"Why didn't she phone Mom or me?"

"I can't answer that, sir."

René was convincing, but neither David nor I believed him.

I didn't want to hurt his feelings so I dropped the subject and said to David, "You look tired and you have lost weight."

"We did so much in so little time. The trip was really hectic. Dr. Taylor was sick from day one. I'm glad he was able to take me around and introduce me to the hospital staff despite how he was feeling. He told the staff that I would be taking over his place, and if ever there was a problem, they should contact me.

"After seeing all the work that was ahead of me, I wanted to tell Dr. Taylor that I didn't think I was ready to undertake such a task. But when I looked into the eyes of some of those helpless people, I decided to at least give it a try.

"A couple of retired doctors were visiting from The States. They run free clinics. I suggested to Dr. Taylor that he should let one of them check him over, but Dr. Taylor said to me, 'Nothing is wrong with me. Why do I need a doctor? I am a doctor and I know what is wrong with me.'

"He barely got through the last couple of days of our visit. He struggled to climb the stairs to get on the plane. At one point I suggested a wheelchair and he nearly chewed my head off.

"The first thing I'm going to do tomorrow is call his friend Dr. Dorothy Newman. She and Dr. Taylor are good friends. They graduated from medical school around the same time. He might listen to her."

"Can I get you something to eat, David?" I asked

"Thank you, Mom, I ate on the plane. Dr. Taylor didn't have a thing to eat from the time we left Calcutta to the time we arrived in Toronto. You know how much he likes his brandy, but he never even touched a drink. He seemed so tired. He slept all the way home."

"You look pretty tired yourself, Sir," René said. "Can I make you a cup of tea?"

"You read my mind, René."

René made a pot of tea and as he was pouring us each a cup he said, "Now that we know Miss Arshana is in Guyana, can something be done to bring her back here?"

"Are you sure she called from Guyana, René?" David asked.

"I am not 100% sure sir, but the voice sounded distant. Maybe because she was crying. There are so many days when I blame myself. No one knows, but I was the one who encouraged her to ask Ma'am for work. I told her not to mention it and she never did."

"Did you know her before?" David asked.

"One day I came here to plant the rosebushes and when I was about to close the gate I noticed that Flossy was restless. I calmed him down and as I did so, I looked across the field and saw a visitor. Despite my fading eyesight, I saw that it was a beautiful young woman, her long hair was blowing in the wind as she walked in my direction.

"As she got closer to me, she stopped and smiled. But I could see that she was frightened. We spoke for a while and then she said, 'Let me show you how to plant those roses. When I was a little girl I always helped my grandmother in her garden. I was more of a nuisance than a help, but I learned how to grow flowers. And you are never going to believe this, but my grandmother spoke to her flowers and she swore they understood her.'

"Flossy who barks at the sight of strangers kept wagging his tail. He looked at her and then at me. I decided there was no harm in letting her help with the roses if I was watching her the whole time.

"As we began to dig, she told me she was looking for work, and I told her how kind you are, Ma'am.

"I miss her very much. I looked forward to coming to work each day and hearing her say, 'René there is still plenty of coffee in the pot, take a break.'

"Before she came, I was thinking about whether to return to El Salvador, but now I think I will. I miss her. I really miss her."

"I know what you mean, René," David said and he got up. Sadness was like a blanket around him.

"I'm going to phone Mrs. Taylor now to see how Dr. Taylor is doing and after that I'm going straight to bed. The jet lag is killing me. I can barely keep my eyes open. I'll tell you both about my trip tomorrow morning. Good night," he said and left.

20

That night, I woke up suddenly to the sound of the phone ringing. I got out of bed and looked at my watch. It was three o'clock in the morning, who could be calling at this hour?

When I picked up the phone, I heard Mrs. Taylor's voice on the other end of the line.

"Sorry to disturb you at this ridiculous hour, Ruth, but there is no one else for me to turn to. Can I speak to David?"

"I'm on the extension line," David said. "It's Dr. Taylor, isn't it, Becky?"

"Yes David. He can hardly breathe and he's complaining of chest pains. He is sitting on the edge of the bed and bending over. It looks as though he's in great pain. He won't allow me to call the ambulance. David, you are the only one who he might listen to."

"Okay, Becky. Just relax. I will be over at your place as soon as I can."

David hung up and I asked him, "Would you like me to come to the hospital and sit with Mrs. Taylor?"

"She would appreciate that, Mom. Right now she needs someone to be with her."

Both David and I got dressed in no time, and since there was no traffic we got to Dr. Taylor's house in within minutes. David had phoned the ambulance on our way over, so the paramedics arrived before we did.

Dr. Taylor was sitting on the bed with his head bent. When he heard us enter he looked up and said to David, "What are you doing here? I am not ready for the grave yet, and I'm not going to the hospital."

David said, "Now come on, let the paramedics do their job. Don't be stubborn, you are going to the hospital and I am accompanying you in the ambulance."

"What about Becky?"

"Don't worry about Becky. Mom is with her. She will drive her to the hospital."

He continued to put up a struggle, but eventually David and the paramedics got him in the ambulance. He was taken directly to the intensive care unit and Becky and I sat and watched as several doctors went to and from his room.

For almost two hours I sat and watched, holding Becky's hand at times when she was shaking. I knew that the doctors were doing everything humanly possible to save Dr. Taylor, but in the end it wasn't enough.

David, accompanied by the chief surgeon, came out of the unit. The surgeon went straight to Becky and said, "I don't know how much of a consolation this will be for you, Mrs. Taylor, but we did our best. Dr. Taylor did not recover consciousness."

Becky stared at David and then at the doctor. She showed no emotions. She was a small and delicate woman, and she looked even more fragile as she sat motionless in her grief.

"Becky," David said as he held her hands and raised her up, "now you go home with Mom. Leave all the worrying and the necessary arrangements to me."

"Maybe I should go to my home," Becky said.

"Now Becky," David asked, "do you know who is in charge of you now?" He placed his arms around her and lifted her chin. "I want you to go to my home with my mom."

"David, you are now in charge of me," she said. She said sadly, "That's what he wanted isn't it? He didn't want me to be with strangers."

"So you have no choice but to listen to me," David smiled.

"What will happen to me now, David?"

"Nothing is going to happen to you, Becky. I will always be there for you. All you have to do is let me know what you want."

And to me he said, "I'll take you both home. See that Becky gets some rest. I'll phone Dr. Fine and we will make arrangements."

I whispered in David's ear, "Dr. Taylor's wishes were that he should be cremated as soon as possible, and that the funeral should be very private. He wanted only Reverend Thomas, Becky, David, Dr. Nancy Fine and myself to be present."

"I know, Mum. He told me that," David said in softly. "I knew this was coming. He was winding up his affairs."

At the funeral, five days later, Reverend Thomas said, "May God be with you, my dear friend. You lived a life that was fruitful and meaningful. You served humanity."

As David led Becky away, she said to him, "David, do you know what Don requested for his ashes?"

"Yes, Becky."

"I won't be making another trip to India, so I will keep the ashes until you can make your next trip to India and scatter Don's ashes over the Ganges."

"I'll miss Don," Becky said. There was so much pain in her voice. "Now take me home, David."

"You're going home with me, Becky," David said.

"No. I am not going to be a burden on you and your mother."

"You are not a burden," David said. He put his arms around her and kissed her forehead, saying, "Don't forget who your boss is now Becky."

"I won't David, I won't."

Becky stayed with us for more than a month and then one morning she said "David I'm not going back to my home. There are too many memories of my Don. I want you to sell my house. I don't know if I am making the right decision, but in this life we have to take chances. I am prepared to take whatever comes my way. David, I want you to buy me one of those beautiful condominiums on Lake Ontario; one with a good view of the lake. In the morning I want to sit in the solarium and watch the dawn breaking."

"As you wish, Becky," David said.

Don's house was sold quickly and fortunately for Becky, the new owners who had just migrated to Canada decided to take the house with all its furnishings. Becky only kept a few pieces that had sentimental value. It was as if Don was watching over Becky, because in less than two weeks, David found her a beautiful condominium with the view of the lake, just as she desired. With the help of Dr. Fine and an interior decorator, Becky was able to move into her new home a couple of months after her husband's death.

It was hard for David to deal with all the responsibilities that were thrust upon him after Dr. Taylor's death. But luckily for him, Dr. Fine and the entire staff put their heads together and helped him out.

Nonetheless, when it came to Arshana, no one could help David. He declined nearly all invitations to parties and often I would see him sitting by the window in the living room, staring blankly at the snow-covered fields. It was a very sad time in his life and I prayed every day that, regardless of the consequences, he would eventually find peace and happiness once again.

21

Two days before my birthday, Ramona phoned to say that she had arranged a little family get-together to celebrate the occasion. "You have all the space in the world, so we will do it at your house."

"But Ramona, this is so sudden and I'm not sure whether I'm in the mood for a party right now."

"If you are worried about the food and drinks, forget it. I have it all arranged with a client of mine who has a catering business. He will provide everything. Even the cake and your favorite roses."

"Ramona, why did you put yourself through all this unnecessary trouble?"

"It's no trouble, Auntie Ruth. You'll never be 60 again and it is the least that I can do for you. All my life you've been there for me. And now I'm going to let you in on a little secret that I've kept to myself for years: when I was a little girl, I often wished that you were my mother. To this day, I have moments when I wish the same. So all I'm asking you to do is sit back and relax. I'll get back to you later."

It was easy for her to tell me to sit back and relax. How could I?

On my birthday, the phone rang all morning. "Everyone seems to remember your birthday," David said as he walked into the kitchen.

"Happy birthday," he said and kissed me. "Of all the days I could have overslept. I should have been in the office an hour ago. Good thing the phone woke me up."

"I'll make you some breakfast," I said.

"No time for breakfast," he said. "But I'll have a quick coffee with you and then I have to run. I'll be home as soon as I can."

After he left, René poured me another cup of coffee and one for himself. As we was sipping our coffee and chatting, René said, "Ma'am, look at that cupboard door, it is falling off the hinges. I'm going downstairs to bring up my toolbox and fix it right away."

"That door was never fixed properly when I renovated the kitchen last year. So René, whilst you fix the door, I'll run some errands and get ready for my party. Unless you would like me to stay and hold the door for you?"

"No Ma'am, you go and look after your bills. If I need help, I'll call you."

I nodded and sat down to write a few outstanding cheques. As I wrote, I heard René hammering away in the kitchen. About an hour later, he rushed into the living room and said, "Ma'am, you probably couldn't hear the phone. It never stopped ringing so I picked it up. A woman's voice on the other end of the line asked to speak to Mrs. Weissman. It sounded urgent. Maybe it is someone calling to tell you something about Miss Arshana. She is still on the line."

"Okay, René, if it will make you happy, I'll come to the kitchen and answer the phone."

"Mrs. Weissman speaking," I said into the receiver.

"Mrs. Weissman, we have never met. You don't know me but if it is at all possible, I would like to come and see you today. It is important that I speak to your husband."

As René had said, the voice seemed desperate.

"Who are you?" I asked.

"My name is Michelle Mason. I'm a dentist from Ohio and for the past two years I have been working in India at Dr. Taylor's leprosy hospital. I'm going to India soon and my co-worker in India, Dr. Sinha, suggested that I get in touch with your husband before I leave. I was hoping that your husband would spare me a moment of his time today."

"Are you in Ohio?"

"No, Mrs. Weissman. I just got to Canada. I'm in Oakville. I have your address. Dr. Sinha emailed it to me along with your telephone number. And I do know Mississauga. I have driven around there several times, so it should be no problem for me to find your place."

"Alright," I said. "May I ask what make of car you are driving? I need to be able to identify you."

"Honda Civic."

René was still sitting at the kitchen table, so I said to him, "A young woman is on her way here, maybe we should go into the living room and watch out for her car. She is driving a Honda."

Fifteen minutes later we saw a Honda driving slowly along the street. "That's her car," René said. "She's probably reading the numbers on the houses."

"Yes, you're right, René, she's turning into our driveway."

A very tall and elegant looking woman stepped out of the car.

"Michelle?" I asked, popping my head through the window.

"Yes, Mrs. Weissman."

"Wait a minute."

René put Flossy in another room and opened the gate.

"Come on up," I said.

She wasn't so elegant looking when I saw her up close. Her hair was tied back in a ponytail and she was wearing faded jeans and runners.

"Have a seat," I said to her. "You must be tired and hungry after having driven all the way from Ohio."

"Not really, I do a lot of driving. It took just over four hours to get here. And when I crossed the border at Niagara Falls, I stopped at a restaurant and had something to eat. But if it isn't too much trouble, I wouldn't mind a cup of tea.

"Mrs. Weissman, I hope your husband can forgive me for barging in on him like this, but I didn't have much of a choice. You see, before I left for South America, I reserved my plane ticket for my trip to India, and only when I returned home the day before yesterday and read my email did I learn that Dr. Taylor had died. Dr. Sinha was the person who emailed me and suggested that I should not return to India unless I spoke to Dr. Weissman. Mrs. Weissman, please believe me, when I learned of Dr. Taylor's death, my whole world turned upside down. Working for Dr. Taylor was my vocation. I finally felt like I was doing something important. And now it seems that my happiness was only short-lived."

"Why is that?" I asked.

"For one thing, Dr. Sinha does not like Americans and I doubt he likes me. In fact, I believe he despises me. I understand that your husband is in charge now, so I hope he will allow me to continue with my work in India."

She seemed genuine enough to me, so after listening to her for a while, I said, "I believe you are here to see my son, not my husband. He's normally home at this time but something must've kept him back."

René, who had been eavesdropping, appeared with a pot of tea.

Young ladies were never invited to my house after Arshana left. René kept a straight face as I introduced him to Michelle.

"No one makes a better cup of tea than René," I said.

"I learned from the best," he replied.

I knew he was referring to Arshana.

"This is a really nice cup of tea," Michelle said to René.

"Thank you," René said as he refilled her cup.

"Tell me something about your work in India, Michelle," I said.

"Working in India has changed my life. After I graduated from dental school, I went gallivanting around the globe, looking for something constructive to do with my life. By chance, one night I ran into Dr. Taylor at a hotel boutique in Calcutta. He was buying a pashmina shawl for his wife. I stood and watched as the saleswoman quoted him $800 for the shawl. As he was about to pay her, I said, 'Just a minute, give her $400 only. If she doesn't want it, I'll take you to another shop. She's charging you almost double the price.' The saleswoman looked at me as though she was ready to kill me and said, 'Excuse me Madam, this is a fixed-price shop. There's no bargaining here. The shawls that are sold here are one-of a-kind. You can search from one end of Calcutta to the other and you would never find shawls like the ones in my store.'

"'Thank you for your time,' I said to her, 'But we're going to try a couple more fixed-price shops.'

"'Okay, Okay' she said, 'I'll give it to you for $600 and not a rupee less. I am losing money.'

"'We don't want you to lose money. So have a good day,' I said. As we turned to walk out of the shop, she began to mumble in Bengali and said, in English, 'You have cut my throat, take it for $400.'

"'You better be careful what you are saying,' I told her.

"'Do you understand Bengali?' the woman asked.

"'I teach Bengali,' I replied.

"She quickly wrapped the shawl, handed it to us, and we paid her and left.

"When we got out of the store, Dr. Taylor asked me how well I spoke Bengali.

"'I don't know a single word,' I said. 'I just know how to deal with boutique owners, not only in India but all over the world. They can spot a tourist a mile away, and if you are an American, heaven help you.'

"Dr. Taylor asked me where I was staying and when he learned that I was staying in the same hotel as he was, he invited me to dinner.

"Over dinner he asked me what I was doing in India and I told him I was in Dubai and just visiting India.

"And when I asked him what he was doing in India, he told me all about his leprosy hospital.

"'If you don't mind, I'd like to do some volunteer work, I'm a dentist,' I said to him.

"'You will never be able to work under the conditions here,' he said.

"'Just try me,' I said. 'I'll go with you and if I don't like it, I could always leave.'

"I have been blessed with everything a person could desire, so I decided to give back to those less fortunate than I. I liked it and I have never regretted working there. It's exactly what I have been searching for all my life.

I was educated in private schools in Europe and at my father's insistence my brother and I were sent to Northwestern University where we both graduated as dentist. My brother, along with his wife Catherine, have a large dental practice in Ohio. When I am not in India, I work with them to keep busy. But I have great plans for the dental clinic in India and I hope that Dr. Weissman will approve of me."

"You can ask him yourself," I said. David had just come inside. "David, I didn't hear your car."

"I parked on the street," he said. "There is a car parked in the middle of the driveway."

"David," I said, introducing them, "this is Michelle. She runs Dr. Taylor's dental clinic in India."

"Yes, I was at the dental clinic when I was there."

"So what are you doing here?" David asked, "Just visiting?"

"No, I'm on my way to India. I needed to get in touch with you before I left, now that you're in charge of the hospital. I work with Dr. Sinha, and even though we don't always see eye to eye, I thought I should listen to him when he told me to come talk to you. Dr. Weissman, I would like to know if I will be allowed to continue my work at the hospital."

David said, "I know nearly all the doctors do voluntary work. I believe that the nurses and a few technicians receive a small salary."

"Dr. Weissman," she said, "do you think I'm suggesting that you pay me? I don't need your money or anyone else's money. I was fortunate enough to get a good inheritance from my grandfather. So I don't ever have to work if I don't want to. You said you visited the dental clinic when in India, but I'm sure you didn't know that all the equipment there was funded by me."

"That is good of you," David said. "Dr. Taylor spoke highly of you. You do want to continue your work in India, don't you?"

"More than anything else, Dr. Weissman."

"Well, I suggest you try and work with Dr. Sinha," David said. "I have met him and from the little I saw of him, I thought he was a very dedicated man. Anyway, I will speak to him as soon as I can and see what the problem is."

"Where are you staying, Michelle?" I asked.

"I usually stay in one of the hotels by the airport. They keep my car for me as long as I want."

"We are having a little get-together here tonight. You can spend the night here if you'd like," I said.

"I've taken up enough of your time, I don't think I should impose myself on you any longer."

"It is no imposition," David said. "My mother has invited you to stay. So if there is no one waiting for you at your hotel, you are free to do as you please. I would like to go to my room and freshen up, so if you want to stay, give me your keys. I'll move your car and bring up your bags."

She handed him her keys and said, "All I need is my overnight bag. It is lying on the front seat of the car." When David left, she asked: "Is he always so bossy?"

"Most of the time," I said. "And believe me, he gets away with it."

When David returned with her bag, I told him to take it to the guest room.

"You may want to shower and have a quick lie down, so let me show you to your room. You should find everything you need," I said. "If not, I am two doors away, just tap on the door. I have to get dressed. The folks should be arriving any time soon. You don't have to hurry down. Take your time. Rest a bit and you can join the party later."

About an hour later, when I was dressed, I went downstairs and found that David was already dressed and standing by the window. He was wearing navy blue slacks and a cream-colored sweater. It was the sweater Arshana and I had bought for him for his birthday. He looked a little bit like his old self.

"Dressed already?" I asked.

"Glad I am, Ramona and Brian just turned into the driveway."

Ramona came waltzing through the front door and David went over to help her.

"Happy birthday, Auntie Ruth," she called out breezing in and perfuming the air all around her. "Let me give you a kiss, Auntie Ruth." And to David she said, "You look as though you could do with a kiss too."

When she kissed him, David asked, "Still wearing cheap perfume?"

"For your information, this cheap stuff set me back $300."

"You could have fooled me," David said.

"I know what it is, David. You want to have a better sniff," and she moved in to hug him once again.

"I would like to take you up on your offer, but your husband is coming up the stairs, and the caterers are trying to find the entrance downstairs."

"I'll run down and show them in."

Ramona had said the caterers were experienced and well-organized. In no time at all they had the buffet table set up and the food all laid out on silver platters. By the time they were through, the guests had started arriving. After the usual hugging and kissing and everyone wishing me a happy birthday, they all went straight for the bar.

In all the excitement, I had completely forgotten Michelle, but apparently she had no problem finding the party room downstairs. She glided into the room looking stunning and confident.

For a moment I almost did not recognize her. She was wearing an impeccably tailored blue dress that matched her blue eyes. Her hair, which was in a ponytail when she arrived, now fell loosely over her shoulders. On her feet she wore sandals which were definitely purchased in India.

Briefly she paused and looked across the room. I thought she was looking for me, then her eyes lit up as she saw David standing across the room. All eyes were on her as she walked towards David. I saw that wicked twinkle in David's eyes and I knew he was enjoying the discomfort and curiosity of everyone present. I hate to admit that I was enjoying it too.

"Hi, come and sit with Mom," he said, bringing her over to my table.

"What can I get you to drink?" David asked her.

"Scotch on the rocks, please."

When he returned with the drink he said, "Hi folks, I just remembered my manners. Meet Michelle Mason. She is a dentist from Ohio and she's one of the many doctors who work in our hospital in India."

Carl was sitting at the table next to me, so he turned his chair around and asked David "You sure this young lady's a dentist? Have you checked her credentials?"

"Haven't had time yet, Uncle Carl. I met her for the first time a couple of hours ago."

Eric, who was sitting at our table, said to Michelle, "Do you by any chance know a Dr. Errol Mason?"

She smiled and said, "I do. Believe me, there are times when I wish I didn't. He happens to be my father and I love him to death."

"A couple of days ago, a friend let me read one of his latest books," Eric said. "I can't wait to tell my friend who I met."

"Is everyone hungry?" Ramona called out. "The food is all laid out, come and help yourselves."

Michelle turned to David and said, "I'm starving."

"Then let's go to the buffet table."

When they returned to our table, Cynthia, who was sitting at the other table, said to David, "I don't think you could've gotten any more food on your plate."

"I can eat as much as I want," David said, "But unfortunately you can't, so sit and be quiet and let me and my guest enjoy our food."

"David, come a little closer, I want to ask you something," Cynthia said.

"Would you stop bugging me, Cynthia?"

"Answer me this one question and I will not bother you again: Can she help you to forget Arshana?"

"No one can ever help me forget her," David replied. He had lost the smile and the desire to continue with his usual banter.

Michelle said, "The food is delicious. I'm going for a second helping." And she got up and walked to the buffet table.

"Cynthia," I said, "I've been listening to you. Behave yourself."

"I am not doing anything, Auntie Ruth. I'm just trying to warn David. That one over there is big trouble," she said. "Everyone here tonight can see that she's after David. Look, she's talking to Brian but she's looking straight over here at David."

"Cynthia, be quiet," David said. "This is not funny any more. Would you like some cake, Mom?"

"No, I'm tired. I'm going to offer my thanks to Ramona and disappear. I have an awful headache."

I don't know how long the party went on after that. I went straight to my room and fell asleep almost immediately.

The next morning when I went down to the kitchen, I saw Michelle and David having coffee.

"Want some breakfast, Michelle?" I asked.

"No thank you, I never eat in the morning," she said. "I was just waiting to thank you for your hospitality. And I thoroughly enjoyed the party last night. I've got to go and get my car before noon, so once again, thank you. Please ask me over again."

"Anytime."

"Perhaps on my way back from India," she suggested. Then she kissed both David and I and picked up her bags.

David said to her, "Give me your bag." He took her bag and walked her to her car. When he returned I asked if he wanted breakfast.

"No," he said, "but I'll have another cup of coffee."

Over coffee he said to me, "I didn't want to tell her, but she's doing a fantastic job in India. As you would have observed, she's quite sure of herself. When I spoke to him the last time, Dr. Sinha said that she's very bossy and she likes things done her way.

"I realize that she has spent thousands of dollars of her own money on the dental clinic. Perhaps Dr. Sinha isn't aware of that. But regardless, I'm not prepared to take sides. India has certain rules and she has to abide by them. Remind me to phone Dr. Sinha tonight, I have an important meeting."

"Alright, see you later this evening," I said, as he left.

22

I was sound asleep when I was awoken by the continuous ringing of the telephone. Half asleep, I picked it up. The voice on the other end was familiar, so I jumped out of the bed to make sure that I was not dreaming. "Who is this?" I asked

"It's Arshana."

"Arshana! Arshana, where are you?"

"Not very far away from your place, Mom. Seems as though I woke you up. I'm so sorry."

"I was just about to get up anyway."

"Mom, I am calling about my passport. I was wondering if you have seen it."

"Yes I have, and I kept it safe for you."

"Would it be convenient if I came around eleven o'clock this morning to collect it? I know you are usually busy on Saturdays. I won't stay very long."

"You can stay as long as you like. I am going out this evening but I'm more or less free for the rest of the day."

"See you soon," she said and hung up.

Still shaking from the sudden shock of hearing her voice, I steadied myself and walked slowly towards David's room. He was still asleep, but when he heard me, he turned around and opened his eyes.

"You're not going to believe this," I said to him, "but I just received a phone call from Arshana."

"From Arshana? Where is she?" he asked, sitting up and wide awake.

"I really don't know. But from what I gather, she is somewhere close by. She will be here at eleven o'clock to pick up her passport and it is almost ten o'clock now. We should hurry and get showered and dressed."

Half an hour later, David and I were sitting in the living room sipping our coffee when a taxi pulled up in our driveway. Arshana stepped out of the taxi, paid the driver and walked gracefully up the stairs. Neither David nor I could believe our eyes when she walked through the door. She looked stunning.

"Hello Mom," she said, and she bent down and kissed me. I got a whiff of expensive perfume. "Hello David. I didn't expect to find you home on a Saturday. I thought that neither you nor René would be around."

"Have a seat, Arshana," I said.

She sat on the edge of a chair and for a while no one spoke.

Breaking the silence, David said, "How could you be so heartless? For a while, Mom and I didn't know what had happened to you. We didn't know whether you were dead or alive until René told us that he had received a call from you in Guyana. How could you do what you did to us? Walk out of here without saying a word?"

She sat motionless, staring at David incredulously. She tried to appear cool and collected, but her cheeks were turning red. She sighed, worked her jaw a little and gazed into David's eyes. Her face was now flushed with embarrassment and I saw that she was trembling. She took a deep breath.

"Could I have gone to Guyana without my passport?"

The question was meant for both David and I.

"We read in the papers," David said, "that your friends were picked up and thrown in jail. We thought that you were deported along with them. I made enquiries but couldn't find out anything."

"Well you thought wrong," she said. "Don't say those things about my friends. They were there for me when I needed them. Where were you?" Her eyes filled with tears and she looked reproachfully at David.

"Arshana, just answer me one question," I asked, "were you in Mississauga for all these months without ever trying to get in touch with us?"

"I was in Mississauga all right. In fact, not too far from here. Mom, can you remember the very first time I came here and asked you for work? You were so worried about trusting me. And I told you not to worry. I promised you that I would never humiliate you. That promise nearly cost me my life. I was pregnant and I had no one to turn to. Often, I was accused by your friends of trying to trap David and get his money, so I did not want them to get the satisfaction of thinking they were right.

"I was so scared to do the operation. But both Mrs. Eisner and Mrs. Nadler helped me to make up my mind. A couple of nights before I left, they were over here playing cards. They abused and insulted me all night.

"At one point Mrs. Nadler said, 'Ruth, why do you still have this girl here? Trust me, she is going to get herself pregnant and David, being the gentleman he is, will be forced to marry her. When she takes over, you will be forced to leave your house.'

"Mom, you sat and listened to them without saying one word in my defense."

"Arshana, they were drunk and if I said anything to them, it would have made matters worse."

"Two days later I went to have the abortion, but I didn't have it. I fainted and the next thing I knew, I was in the hospital with no clue as to how I got there. I was in a hospital bed and a woman was standing over me. She was smiling down at me and she had the most sympathetic eyes that I had ever seen.

"'Did you have a good night's rest? Are you ready to go home?' she asked me.

"I told her, 'I have no home, no family or money or place to go.'

"She said that the people who checked me in had told her about my attempted abortion. But she didn't judge me. She told me her name was Paula and she said, 'Now tell me Arshana, why would a girl like you try to do something so terrible to an unborn child?'

"I told her I had no choice and that I didn't know who the father was. But she said, 'I believe you do know, Arshana, but you want nothing more to do with him, am I right?'

"'Yes you are,' I said.

"Paula said, 'Arshana, since you have no place to go, I'll make you an offer. I have an apartment that isn't very far from here and I can let you stay there until your baby is born. Everything would be provided for you and no one would ever disturb you. When your baby is born, if it is alright with you, my husband Robert and I will adopt it. I'm trusting you not to take advantage of the help I'm offering.'

"I told her that I was brought up to be honest and that I would accept her offer under one condition: She couldn't ask any questions. She gave me her word that she wouldn't ask me anything.

"Paula paid my hospital bill and took me to her apartment. I grieved and suffered in silence but with the passing of each day I became closer and closer to Paula and her husband Robert. They enjoyed my cooking and several nights during the week they would stay over and have dinner with me. Robert is a real estate developer and employs more than 60 people. Almost immediately I was put on his payroll so I had all the money I needed throughout my pregnancy. Paula and Robert were there for me and when Bobby was born, I had him in my arms for a few minutes before handing him over to Paula. Robert waited outside and according to Paula, when Bobby was placed in his arms, tears came rolling down his cheeks.

"I had to give my child away, but when I looked at Paula and Robert and the joy in their eyes, I was happy; although I was in agony, I knew that I had given him to two adoring people who would love him all his life."

"Arshana, you could've come to us for help," I said.

"Would you have accepted a bastard grandson? Neither of you ever defended me."

"Arshana, I defended you as much as I could," David said. "But my hands were tied. Over and over and over again I begged you to marry me but you refused. What more could I have done? Time and again I told you that I wanted you as my wife; not only someone to cook and do the dishes. As my wife, no one would have said a word against you."

Arshana ignored David and said to me, "You know how many times I picked up the phone and wanted to call you, Mom? But I didn't want you to judge me as your friends often did.

"During the last week of my pregnancy, I was so depressed. I came to the house and saw René's car in the driveway. I did not want him to see me in my pitiful condition. René loved and respected me and I didn't want him to be disappointed in me. From there I went over to your office, David. I didn't want to go, but I was at the very lowest point in my life and I wanted help and advice. I did not want to cause you any embarrassment, so I waited in a coffee shop across from the medical building and waited for you. I tried calling a couple of times but on both occasions I was told to leave a message. I must've sat for over an hour and lo and behold I saw you coming out of your office looking happy as a lark with your arm around one of your nurses. You passed so close to the window, you could have touched the glass. Of course you were too preoccupied to notice me. A month later my son was born. A couple of weeks afterwards, Robert and Paula took me into the lawyer's office for me to sign the adoption papers.

"The lawyer, an elderly gentleman told Paula and Robert to give me more time to think things over. That night I went home and thought about it all night long. The next morning I got up and went to your office. I phoned and was told that you would be leaving the office shortly and would not be back until the following day. It was lunch time and I thought you were on your way to lunch. Five minutes later you came out of the office holding hands with a woman. I presume she was a doctor because she was wearing a stethoscope around her neck. I followed you to the parking lot and what I saw made me make up my mind right away.

"Later that evening I called Robert and told him that I was prepared to sign whatever papers he had for me. The next day when we went to the lawyer's office I told Robert that he could put himself down as the father and I would verify it. As I was signing the papers, the lawyer told me that I really should have a lawyer of my own.

"I asked him what for and he said, 'Young lady, you are too honest and trusting. Never ever be too trusting. However, I will make sure that you are taken care of for the rest of your life. To begin with, one million dollars will be put in your account and there will be lots more to follow.'

"I told him I was already being paid a monthly salary for work I did not do. And I asked him 'What would I do with a million dollars?'

"He told me 'I once read that a woman can never be too thin or too rich.

"And then I named the baby 'Robert' after his father and grandfather. It did cross my mind to call him David, but on second thought I realize that you would want that name reserved for your son."

Then Arshana turned to me and said, "Mom, if you think back to when you were in Guyana, my grandmother told you she could see my future. She told me the same; that I was going to go through a very unhappy period in my life, then find happiness forever. Well, that unhappy period is over and I'm content."

"I hope you're happy," David said. "You sold our son. But I promise you, you're not going to get away with what you did."

"You can't do a damn thing, David," Arshana said. "And I'm warning you, don't try anything stupid, you will regret it. You may think that you have a lot of money but Paula and Robert Romano have ten times more. The man that I marry one day will have fifty times more. Not to mention his power and influence. Remember you would have to face me in court. Trust me, you wouldn't want me to testify against you. Do you remember my friends Sita and Rita? You know they were deported. Well they would love to return to Canada and testify against you. You are thinking of playing rough, but I would think twice if I were in your shoes."

It tore me apart to hear her talk like that. I felt terrible for all she went through but she had changed so much and I knew that nothing I said would appease her. I still had to try.

"Arshana, I know there must be anger between you and David, please don't take it out on us. I can't remember ever being unkind to you. I don't want to speak for David but I could see he loved you. I saw how jealous he was when you received all that attention from men wherever you went. It dawned on me that your feelings for each other were turning into love. I didn't want to interfere. I kept waiting for either of you to say something to me, but neither of you did. Had I known that you were pregnant, I would have stepped in.

"Arshana, I am not taking sides, but David suffered a lot when you left. For hours he would stand by the window and gaze at the open fields. And he would walk over to your room and stand outside the door. He went through hell."

"Arshana," David said, "I'm begging you, I'm willing to pay the Romanos any amount of money they ask for, if they would return my son."

"And once again, I am telling you David, Bobby is not your son. And the Romanos don't need your money. They have more right to Bobby than you do. During the last month of my pregnancy, when it was so frustrating for me, the Romanos stood by me. Paula spent the last month off work to be with me. She saw how depressed I was, and neither she nor Robert wanted me to be alone in that apartment. They feared that I would have done something to myself. I didn't. Thank God I survived."

"Arshana," David said, "how could you become so heartless? You are not the person I once knew."

"I'm definitely not the person you once knew. No one can kick me around anymore." She was now bubbling over with anger. She looked stricken, but she quickly composed yourself.

"You accuse me of being heartless. I wasn't heartless, I was helpless. I was unable to look after myself, so how could I have looked after the child? So I did what I had to do. And now as I look back, I thank God that I made the right decision. My decision may affect and hurt you both but I have no regrets and I'm prepared to live with the consequences. My child is well taken care of by two adoring parents, four grandparents and two nannies who will love and adore him. I could never have provided him with what he has now."

"But I could have," David said. "We could."

"Unfortunately, you are busy elsewhere," she replied. "I wanted to hurt you the same way I was hurt. My anger is my defence against the pain you caused me. Revenge is the only sane action, and believe me, it won't be long before I get back at a few people."

Then, looking down at her watch, it was as if Arshana snapped out of her anger. She said, "I did not expect to be here so long. I have to go now."

She opened her purse and took out a small cell phone, causing a picture from the purse to fall to the ground. It was a picture of a smiling baby, all dimples and no teeth. David picked up the picture, looked at it for a while and handed it to me.

"He looks exactly like you, Arshana," I said.

"Arshana," David said, "I want you to answer this question: How the hell would Mom and I have known that you were pregnant? If you wanted us to feel guilty to ease your conscience, you have succeeded. Is there any other terrible thing we have done that you forgot to mention?"

"I am in a hurry. I have to go."

She then walked briskly towards the door. David walked ahead of her, blocked the door and took the phone away from her. She hit him with her purse and said, "Give me my phone and get out of the way." And turning to me, she said, "Mom would you ask him to get out of the way and return my phone?"

"David," I said, "you have no right to stop her. Would you please return the phone to her immediately?"

"Thanks Mom," she said.

"Arshana," David said, "I know you. The reason you came here today is because you wanted to speak to both Mom and me."

"Stop dreaming," she said. "Get the hell out of my way."

She hit him a couple more times with her purse. "When I needed you, you were not there. You will never understand what it was like to see the child you carried and suffered with for nine months taken away from you. I died a thousand times." She looked at David and I saw the truth in her eyes. She still loved him.

"Get away from the door," she said.

David moved from in front of the door. He smiled at her, struggling to be polite.

"I'll give you a ride home," he said.

"No thanks," she said and walked down the stairs.

David followed after her. They were yelling at each other, getting louder and louder. And then there was complete silence. I was scared. And when I looked through the window, I saw David driving out of the garage with Arshana sitting beside him.

An hour later, David returned and said to me, "You are not going to believe this, she's staying in the same high rise as Becky."

"David, I hope you have not forgotten, we're supposed to be at Carl and Martha's 35th anniversary party tonight. Cynthia phoned yesterday to remind me."

"I'll go with you to have dinner and then I'll slip away around 11. If I don't come back to get you, ask someone for a ride home."

"David, I am begging you, please don't get yourself into trouble."

"Arshana told me that she was going to a party with those Romanos this evening. She said they normally bring her home before midnight. So I'm going to drive over to the apartment, sit in my car, and wait to see who these people are. And tomorrow I'm going to hire a private detective to find out what he can about them."

23

The next day I sat having my second cup of coffee when it dawned on me that David had not come down for breakfast. I looked at my watch. It was already one o'clock so I went up to his room, peeked in and saw that his bed had not been slept in.

Horrible thoughts crossed my mind. As long as I can remember, he had never ever stayed out all night without phoning me. I wondered if he had gone to Arshana's condo, caused trouble and ended up in jail.

"Oh God, help me," I begged. And like an answer to my prayer, I heard the latch on the front gate click. I dashed into the living room, spilling my coffee. I looked through the window and to my disbelief, I saw David and Arshana walking hand in hand up the stairs. The day before, they were ready to kill each other as they walked down those same stairs.

"You had me so worried, David," I said as he walked through the door.

"Sorry, Mom, I meant to call you, but it got too late and I figured that you would have gone to bed already."

"I can see that the two of you have made up."

"Yes, we are getting engaged. We would like to keep it a secret for now. But I would like to buy Arshana a ring. I'm hoping to go to India soon and I want her to go with me. Robert's lawyer has been working on her immigration papers, and if we get married, it will speed things up."

"I know where I can get really good jewelry," I said. "I'll phone Paul Bernstein. He was a very good friend of your father's. Every piece of jewelry I own was bought from him. Ramona was in his shop a few weeks ago and she did mention that he was inquiring about me. I understand that he only goes to his shop twice a week for a few hours. His youngest son Jacob is looking after the business."

"Is he in Mississauga?" David asked.

"He lives in Mississauga but his business is in downtown Toronto. Just off Queen Street."

"It's a busy area. It's difficult to find parking there," said David.

"We can take the GO train. I can drive Arshana and myself to the station. It would be so much easier than driving downtown."

"I guess you want to go with her to buy the ring," asked David. Arshana looked at him hopefully and he laughed. "Okay, you ladies go to it. That's not really my cup of tea."

The next morning, David picked up Arshana from her apartment and dropped her off at my house before going to work.

"Take the 11 o'clock train," he suggested, "by then the morning rush will be over."

"I spoke to Paul Bernstein last night and he will be waiting for us around twelve o'clock at the shop."

"Well I have to go now," David said. "I'm already late for work. You better hurry if you don't want to miss your train."

"I'm already dressed," I said. "We will leave for the station now."

Arshana and I were just getting into my car when René turned into the driveway.

"Oh, there is René," Arshana said and she ran up to him, hugged him and kissed him. They both began to cry.

"Is that really you, Miss Arshana?" René asked. "Let me have a good look at you. I kept hoping that one day you would return and I can't believe I'm actually looking at you."

"Where are you staying, Miss Arshana?"

"With friends."

"Come on Arshana," I said, "let's go, we don't want to miss our train."

"Where are you going, Ma'am?" René asked.

"René, I'm going to let you in on a little secret. David and Arshana are planning on getting married soon. I'm familiar with one of the jewelry shops downtown so I'm taking Arshana there so she can choose her ring."

"I can take you downtown, Ma'am. I know Toronto like the palm of my hand," René said. "Trust me, I will have no difficulty finding somewhere to park."

"René, I am sure we will miss our train, so I'm going to take you up on your offer, let's go."

There wasn't much traffic on the Queen Elizabeth Way so we got into Toronto in about 20 minutes. René found us a parking spot quite close to the jewelry store in no time.

"It shouldn't take more than an hour, René," I said.

"Ma'am, stay as long as you like, it is a flat-rate. Fifteen dollars."

"What are you going to do in the meantime, René?" I asked.

"Forget about me, Ma'am, take all the time you need. I have not been in downtown Toronto for ages and I would like to look around."

It was only 11:20 when we arrived at Paul Bernstein's shop, but he was already there.

"Hi Ruth, I have not seen you in ages. It is so good to see you. I often think of giving you a call but you know what it is like. You think of something, you get busy and forget. And now Ruth, what can I do for you?"

"I've got my daughter-in-law here to choose a couple of rings."

"These days, there's so much to choose from. It just depends on what you want, Ruth. "Is there anything you have in mind, young lady," he asked Arshana.

"Something very simple," she replied.

"What is your birthstone?" he asked.

"Emerald."

"Good. Last week I received a new shipment of emerald and ruby rings. I can't remember which vault I put them in."

Jacob, Paul's son, was standing close by. He had been watching Arshana from the moment we walked into the store and I could see that it was making her uncomfortable. "They are in the second vault, Dad," he said.

"Then get the tray out, Jacob."

Jacob brought out a tray which was laden with emerald rings."

"What variety," I said. And to Arshana I said, "Choose what you like. There are some beautiful engagement ring and wedding band sets."

Arshana took up a set and she kept turning it around and fiddling with it. My guess was that she was trying to see the price.

"Don't worry about the cost," I whispered to her. "David told me to buy whatever you want."

"Ruth," Paul Bernstein said, "I always remembered that necklace and earring set Solomon bought you several years ago. It was for your 25th wedding anniversary and it was studded with emeralds and diamonds. It was a beautiful piece, handcrafted in the old country. You will never find another set like that. Do you still have it?"

"I do, Paul, and I must have worn that set three times in my whole life."

"If you don't wear it, give it to the young lady as a wedding present. It would match perfectly with the ring she has in her hand."

"She's certainly welcome to have it if she wants it."

"Mom," Arshana said, "I can't take your jewelry."

"Well you can take it now or take it later, Arshana. Eventually it will be all yours."

Arshana was still holding the rings that she had first selected.

"Try them on for size," Paul Bernstein said.

When she tried them on, they were a little too big so Bernstein said, "I'll have them sized and ready in a few days."

"Ruth, why don't you go to the bank tomorrow and take out the emerald set? I can come by your place tomorrow and pick it up to have it cleaned and polished in a week's time. I'll have no trouble returning it to you, I live close by."

"Thanks, Paul. I appreciate that."

"When you wear all that beautiful jewelry you will look like a real Jewish princess," Jacob said to Arshana.

Sensing Arshana's growing discomfort, I told Paul that we had to leave, and we said goodbye.

There was still plenty of time before René had to pick us up so I suggested to Arshana that we go over to the Eaton Centre. There were lots of things on sale. We browsed around for a bit. I stopped at the perfume counter at the Bay and Arshana went over to the men's department.

When I joined her, I saw that she had selected some silk shirts with matching ties. They were already in boxes and she had chosen four of them.

"Both David and Robert have to wear dark coloured suits," she said to me. "These ties and shirts would match perfectly."

After the boxes were wrapped I suggested that we go over to the women's department but she said she really didn't need anything.

"What about shoes?" I asked. "You said you needed some shoes."

"Yes I do, but there's no rush. There are plenty of good shoe stores in Mississauga. In fact, there's a good one quite close to David's office, Mom," she said pleadingly. "I'd like to buy something for you. You have always bought me so many nice things. Remember, I am being paid a salary every month."

"Don't worry, I'll take you up on your offer the very next time we go shopping. In fact I should have offered to pay for the shirts and ties you bought."

"Why? It's my treat for David and Robert."

When we were done, I called René and had him meet us in the parking lot.

"Want to go anywhere else?" he asked.

"No René, let's head home. I want to skip rush hour."

It didn't take us very long to get home and as soon as we turned into the driveway, I knew that Betty was cooking up a storm.

"I wonder what she's cooking," I said.

"We will find out soon enough," René replied. As we entered the kitchen, René said, "Betty, what are you cooking? I'm sure the whole neighbourhood can smell it. You're probably killing Mrs. Chopra with curiosity."

"Leave that poor woman alone, René," Betty laughed.

"He always feels he has to say something terrible about Mrs. Chopra or Gladys," I said. And to Betty I said, "I don't believe you have met Arshana."

"No Ma'am, but there isn't a day that goes by without my hearing her name. The Spanish fella never stops talking about her cooking."

"You can call me whatever you like Betty," René replied. "I'm not going to let you ruin my day, because my favorite people are getting married; David and Miss Arshana."

"Really?" Betty asked.

"Yes, Betty. Now tell me what you're cooking," I said.

"I made a leg of lamb with roast potatoes and carrots. And I am now making lasagna for tomorrow. I'm not sure if I will come to work tomorrow. I have a dentist appointment. I'm getting a root canal and I always feel terrible after those."

"You sure it is a dentist appointment and not your new boyfriend?" René asked.

"Ma'am, would you ask this lazy bum to go and buy me a couple of loaves of Italian bread? I'll make some garlic bread to go along with the lasagna. I'll wrap it in the foil, then all you have to do tomorrow is stick it in the oven."

"René, there's money in the jar over there. Take some out to buy the bread later."

"Anything else you need, Ma'am?" asked René.

"Some ice cream for dessert. Preferably pralines and cream, you know how Arshana loves ice cream."

"You can say that again, Ma'am," René said. "One day I saw her put away a quart of ice cream without coming up for air."

"René," Arshana said, "don't give away my secrets."

Then she asked me, "Mom, should I set the table?"

"Good heavens I didn't realize it was that late. David should be home any moment."

Arshana had just finished setting the table when in walked David. From the moment he walked through the door, I knew he was upset.

"Problems in the office again today?" I asked.

"Yes, we had a staff meeting this afternoon and Dr. Fine walked out and said she was quitting. She's very pigheaded. The office is her life and she puts her heart and soul into seeing that it is well-run. Everyone at the office knows how to deal with her. But there are a couple of female doctors who don't like her and she doesn't like them either. They are the ones causing the trouble.

"I'm the one who has to settle all the disputes and most of the time I find myself between the devil and the deep blue. Sometimes I seriously think of selling the office, but I know that if I did I would be letting Dr. Taylor down. And then there is Becky. The office gives her a bit of happiness. She always refers to the clinic as Don's office and when she visits, she walks around, settles things and even straightens the pictures on the wall. She remembers when and where every picture was bought. Her favorite picture is the one of the two dancing girls. Don bought that picture in India, in Rajasthan. When he brought it home he handed it to Becky and told her that Rajasthani women have the best figures in the world from balancing the pots on their heads. Becky always finishes that story by saying that she threw a hairbrush at Dr. Taylor.

"She has so many precious memories and the office is still her life. I took her out to lunch last Monday and she wept all through it. I can't let her down now. I'll try and manage somehow or the other."

Then David said, "Something smells good. I had no lunch today and I'm very hungry. But I'll run upstairs and take a quick shower."

As he was climbing the stairs, the phone rang.

When he picked it up, I heard him say, "Hello sweetheart, how is the love of my life?"

I didn't know who he was talking to so I quickly looked around to see where Arshana was. She was in the kitchen putting rolls in the oven.

To my relief, I heard him say, "I'm not buttering you up, you know how much I depend on you. 10 years ago when Dr. Taylor introduced us, he told you to keep an eye on me. And by God you have never failed to do so. I am not being sarcastic, Nancy.

"Nancy, you know the heavy burden I have had to carry since Dr. Taylor died, not only here in Canada but in India, and had it not been for you, I would have given up long ago.

"So Nancy, I'm begging you, make it easier for me. At the moment, I'm both mentally and physically exhausted."

I couldn't hear what she said, but I heard David said, "Stop that kind of talk, Nancy. What do you mean by saying that I ought to be physically exhausted? My mother and the young lady I'm getting married to are standing right here."

Nancy Fine said something, and David responded, "Nancy, you listen to too much office gossip. The next Mrs. Weissman is standing right here. If you don't believe me, come over right now and met her... Wait a minute, let we see what Mom has for dinner."

"Plenty of food," I said, "and you are invited, Nancy."

In no time, Doctor Nancy Fine was at the front door.

"Did you fly over here, Nancy?" asked David.

"I tried to get here as fast as I could to kill you. But first let me say hello to your mom." And to Arshana, she said, "This must be the lady David plans to marry. I have met you before. I never forget a beautiful face. It must have been at a party here."

"When is the wedding, David?" Nancy asked.

"As soon as possible," said David. "I'm not losing her again ever."

"Hallelujah! My headache and all your worries will soon disappear," said Nancy. "Tomorrow morning I'm going to walk into the office and let everyone know that I dined the night before with the future Mrs. Weissman. It is going to shake up a few people and I might even be lucky enough to get a few resignations. I'm so happy, I could cry. But before I cry, I could do with a scotch and soda."

"Nancy?" David asked, "How much did you have to drink before you got here?"

"Considering the ordeal I went through in the office this afternoon, I had to have a couple of drinks to calm my nerves."

"I'm glad you have a chauffeur to drive you around," said David.

Then he said to all of us, "Come on. Sit down. Let's eat. I'm so hungry I could eat a horse."

"I'm not serving horsemeat tonight, David," I said. "But there is a leg of lamb accompanied by potatoes and carrots, lasagna, garlic bread and a salad."

As we sat down to eat, Dr. Fine said, "Everything on the table looks so good. I rarely have the pleasure of a home-cooked meal. David, stop stuffing your face and pass me the bread," she said.

"Oh, we have hot rolls in the oven too," Arshana said. "I forgot to take them out."

She then got up, went to the kitchen and brought the rolls. She placed them in front of Dr. Fine.

"Marry this idiot soon, sweetheart," Nancy said to Arshana. "There are a lot of schemers and vultures out there waiting to grab him."

"Nancy, stop exaggerating," David said.

"When I walked out of the office this afternoon, I said to myself, 'Nancy this is one of your worst days.' But it turned out to be one of my best days."

Over dessert she said to me, "Mrs. Weissman this was a very lovely dinner. I would have liked to stay on and enjoy a cup of coffee but I want to go home now and enjoy a good night's sleep. A lot of people might think that I wouldn't show up in the office after a day like today, but I'm going to be there very early. Once again Mrs. Weissman, I thank you for an excellent dinner."

She left shortly after.

24

I had phoned Arshana the night before and invited her to have lunch with me today. I was making vine leaves, a Greek food that was a favourite of David's, and I wanted to show her how to make them. As a little boy, David would sit with me and make dozens of vine leaves. He even helped me roll them.

It was Saturday and David was home so he went and picked up Arshana just after breakfast. I had assembled all the ingredients the night before, so as soon as she arrived, we began making vine leaves.

As we sat and chatted, I asked her whether she was prepared for her wedding.

"More or less; I have bought my dress and shoes, but I'm a bit concerned about where we're going to live after we get married. I know that neither Paula nor Robert would mind if we continued to stay in the apartment but I would rather not."

"Of course not," I said. "I did mention to David that if you both wanted to, you are more than welcome to come and live here with me. This house is far too large for me to live here by myself."

"David did mention it to me, but we never spoke of the details. Mom, I would like nothing better than to live here with you but it wouldn't be fair to either of us. You are only 60, you are in good health and you do a fair amount of entertaining. You need your space."

Arshana continued, "There's a condo for sale near the Romanos' place. It's being sold privately, so you wouldn't see any listings for it in the paper.

"Have you seen the apartment? And do you know the owner?" I asked.

"Yes to both. The owners are Fred and Jackie, friends of the Romanos. When they are in town I usually have lunch or dinner with them.

"Fred and Jackie both have prominent positions in the airline business. Fred is married and has been separated from his wife for about four years. Anna, his wife, left him for a much younger man and let Fred support her financially for years. Now that Fred has decided enough is enough and he's finally getting his divorce, he wants to get rid of the condo rather than hand it over to Anna. Anna doesn't know that Fred owns a condo right now. This is why Fred and Jackie are having a private sale. Knowing that David and I are getting married soon, they are willing to accept an offer from us without starting a bidding war. I told them that I would discuss it with you and David. If you aren't interested, Robert says he will buy it.

"It is a corner unit with a spectacular view of the lake and the best part of the whole deal is that Fred is selling it as-is. All furnishings, drapes, dishes, paintings, the bedroom and dining room sets are included. Jackie and Fred are leaving it all behind and moving to Vancouver.

"Robert said that, for the price they're asking, it's a steal."

David listened to us as we talked and out of the blue he said, "I think it is sad that that marriage has broken up. Sad that he is selling the house without his wife knowing."

He looked at Arshana, "That seems like a sad way of starting our lives. Don't you think? Our child was given away, and now this?"

"How can you say that, David?" Arshana put down her fork and glared at him, her eyes tearing up. "Do you know that I cry every night? Many nights I lie in bed, unable to sleep, and watch the luminous hands of my bedside clock pass from hour to hour, wondering if my baby is awake and crying for me. But thank God he's with parents who love and adore him. No matter what you say, I still don't regret giving him to Paula and Robert.

"I was told that I almost fainted a couple of times during the delivery but recovered quickly when I heard the sound of Bobby's piercing cry. As they took him away to another area to check him over, I could hear him yelling louder and louder, perhaps because he knew that they were taking him away. 'Please don't take him,' I yelled. The doctor had to put his arms on me and calm me down."

The words just spilled out from her. I know she and David tried to avoid that subject, but it was upper most in their minds. Neither of them could stop thinking of their child.

Arshana continued, "For days afterwards, I was sore and weak but Paula and Robert took turns to stay with me. I had plenty of time to think. I felt that the birth of my child changed my life. I prayed more than I had ever prayed before. I even told God that I was angry with him for putting me through all this suffering and then I thought of my very strict upbringing and realized that there was no one else to blame but me. I felt that my suffering was justified because I had sinned. I promised never to make the same mistake again. From that moment on, I felt that my sins were forgiven and all my aches and pains disappeared."

When Arshana finished her speech, tears were flowing from her eyes. I could see that David was beginning to soften up. I knew he was tempted to put his arms around her and comfort her; but they were both very strong-willed people. He just sat and looked at her.

I realized it was time for me to leave them to talk, so I got up, put away the vine leaves we had made and said, "David, Arshana, you are both trying very hard to send me to an early grave, so I am going to leave right now. I have an appointment with my hairdresser which I intend to keep. So, in case I have a heart attack, at least I'll be a pretty corpse in my coffin with my hair all done up." And as I was about to walk through the door I said to Arshana, "Would you tell Fred and Jackie that I'm ready to put down a payment on the apartment? I'm going to buy it."

With that business attended to, I said, "Now talk sensibly you two. This will be a good marriage if you always talk to each other and listen to each other."

They were so similar in nature, so headstrong that it worried me. Yet I knew that they were meant for each other.

25

I woke up in a haze and slowly tried to put my thoughts together. Then I felt a sudden surge of happiness and couldn't think of why. The haze cleared and I realized why I felt so happy: It was the day David and Arshana were getting married.

It is the dream of most couples to have a nice wedding with lots of guests, music and flowers, but David and Arshana chose to have a simple ceremony. I looked at the silver clock on my bedside table and saw that I still had plenty of time to go down to City Hall. I got dressed, went down to the kitchen and made myself a cup of coffee. I was far too excited to have breakfast. After my coffee, I got into my car and headed straight for City Hall.

The only people who knew of the wedding were Paula, Robert and myself. Paula and Robert were already there when I arrived. When they saw me, Paula came up to me and said, "They are not here yet. I hope they have not changed their minds."

Suddenly I had a funny feeling in my stomach. David was always on time, so why wasn't he here yet? But at five to twelve, David and Arshana walked through the huge doors of City Hall holding hands. David looked as though he had just stepped out of a fashion magazine. Wearing a navy blue suit and the cream-coloured shirt and tie that Arshana had bought, he looked more handsome than ever.

Arshana looked stunning. All the swimming exercise she had

been doing since Bobby's birth certainly paid off. The cream-coloured suit she wore fit her slim figure perfectly. She wore very little makeup. The only jewelry she wore was a diamond and emerald encrusted brooch which I had given her as a wedding present.

The ceremony was short, so in less than half an hour, David and Arshana became husband and wife. Paula had made reservations for lunch at a nearby restaurant. The table was reserved, so we were seated as soon as we arrived. Once we were comfortable, our waiter opened a bottle of champagne. We toasted the newlyweds.

The menu that Paula had selected was delicious. We dined on warm lobster bisque and a rack of lamb served with pomegranate mashed potatoes and baby peas. For dessert we were served warm cream brindle with fresh strawberry topping.

After lunch, Paula and Robert went back to work and I went home. David and Arshana returned to their condo, changed into jeans and T-shirts, picked up their bags and drove to the Sheraton Brock at Niagara Falls.

They spent a couple of days there and as soon as he returned, the first person David phoned was Becky Taylor. He told her that he was married and leaving for India soon and his priority was taking Dr. Taylor's ashes to Varanasi. He also spoke to Dr. Fine, told her about the wedding and his trip, and begged her to keep things running smoothly until his return.

The next day, Arshana and David boarded a British Airways flight bound for India.

Meeting them at the airport in India were Ken Campbell and his new bride Kathleen. Kathleen was a dedicated doctor from California who did aid work for tsunami victims. Ken met Kathleen through his father, who volunteered with Kathleen, and they had married two weeks later.

Also at the airport was Arun Chatterjee, a friend of David's from medical school who had studied in Canada and moved back to India afterwards.

Soon enough, David, Arshana, Kathleen, Ken, Arun and Arun's wife Mala, boarded an express train to Varanasi. Mala arranged for a Brahmin priest said a short prayer before scattering Dr. Taylor's ashes into the Ganges. Afterwards, the group returned to the hotel and had time to sample the rose-petal-garnished cocktails before dinner.

The next morning, after a well-deserved rest, they took an early morning flight to Ranchipur and then went on to Indrapur to visit the leper colony and hospital.

On their arrival, they were greeted by a very happy Dr. Sinha and a couple of his coworkers.

After a tea reception, they were taken for a tour around the hospital and the leper colony. Afterwards, David complimented Dr. Sinha on all the improvements he had made since David had last visited with Dr. Taylor.

Dr. Sinha complained about 'that American lady dentist,' and asked Arshana if she too was American. Arshana said, "I am of Indian origin. My forefathers were from Allahabad and they migrated to Guyana many years ago."

Dr. Sinha must have liked her answer because he told anyone who would listen to him, that his new boss's wife was not American, not Canadian, but Indian like them and he knew she would understand their 'ways.' Dr. Sinha took the opportunity to tell Arshana about the need for a children's home, and Arshana promised him that she would see what she could do about fundraising when she returned to Canada.

After spending a few more days visiting the nearby villages, Arun and Mala returned to Calcutta. Before she left, Mala assured David that at least once a month she would visit Indrapur to check on things.

David, Arshana, Ken and Kathleen flew to Mumbai to catch the plane for Canada. The plane was scheduled to leave at midnight so they had a twelve-hour stopover in Mumbai.

Mala had suggested to the ladies that if they wanted to do any shopping in Mumbai, they should go to the Crawford market. The market was designed by Lockwood Kipling, the father of Rudyard Kipling and it had everything money could buy. Arshana and Kathleen shopped all day long. Ken and David had a hard time keeping up with them. By the time they boarded the plane at midnight, they were all so exhausted that they slept until they reached London. They only had a two-hour stopover in London before they changed planes for Toronto.

David phoned me as soon as the group landed and told me not to let anyone else know that they were back. He said the trip had been exhausting and they wanted a couple of days to rest. Ken and Kathleen went on to Ken's home in Oakville.

After resting for a couple of days, David and Arshana's first visitors were Paula and Robert. Naturally they wanted to know everything about the trip and Arshana casually mentioned the need for a children's home. Without any question or hesitation, Paula and Robert agreed to build it. The home was named Bobby Romano's Home, which they named after their son.

26

Every year on the first Friday in December, it was customary for Dr. Taylor to have a staff Christmas party. David decided to continue with the tradition. He invited everyone connected to the clinic; lawyers, accountants, medical and maintenance staff.

The night of the party was a chilly but otherwise perfect December evening. Millions of twinkling stars blazed in the skies and a huge orange moon electrified the entire area. Arshana and I were as happy as all the other women, because there was no snow on the ground, so we were all decked out in designer gowns and open-toed shoes.

Dr. Fine had chosen a fancy hotel for the party. Valet attendants were waiting to park cars as guests arrived and uniformed doormen opened doors and bowed while guests strolled into the foyer.

Huge floral arrangements lined the entrance to the dining room and candles were placed everywhere to create a cozy feeling.

As excited guests entered the dining room, waiters stood with trays in their hands dispensing glasses of champagne.

People were asked to be in their seats at seven o'clock. At half past seven, David walked into the room with pride.

On one arm was Becky Taylor and on the other, Arshana.

Everyone seemed to let out a deep breath all at once. And then there was dead silence. All eyes were now fastened on the two women on David's arms. Arshana walked with grace, wearing a close-fitting emerald green dress encrusted with hundreds of pearls and crystal drops. It matched perfectly with the emerald necklace and earring set that she was wearing. On her hand was a diamond bracelet, a wedding gift from David that glittered and glowed as it caught the light. What a lovely woman she had become. She probably wasn't even aware of how stunning she looked.

I could see that she was a bit nervous, but sitting close to David reassured her that there was nothing to worry about. Sitting at the table was Dr. Nancy Fine, Dr. Ahmad, Robert and Paula, Ken and Kathleen Campbell and myself.

David waited until the speculations, the whispering and the oohs and ahhs had died down, then he took the mic and said "Ladies and Gentleman."

There was an expectant silence.

"First let's honour Dr. Taylor's memory, and all that he did and all that we owe him." He talked for awhile about the clinic and its future and the legacy of Dr. Taylor.

The tension in the room was palpable, and finally, with that wicked twinkle in his eyes, David said, "Since my return from India, I have heard all kinds of gossip and rumours. Well some of it is true and some of it is not. But the one about my being married is true, so I'd like to introduce you all to my beautiful wife, Arshana.

"For over a year, I have been begging her to marry me, but she refused me. Now that we're married, I feel like I'm one of the luckiest men alive."

He looked at Arshana. Her face was radiant with happiness and she smiled at him.

"And now I would like to say something about a very special lady who means a lot to me. Dr. Nancy Fine! When Dr. Taylor died, I was scared of all the responsibilities that were suddenly thrust upon me. But this wonderful lady stepped in and took charge of everything and I have never regretted giving her control. I know she gets help from Dr. Ahmad and he keeps in the background, and I know that all the doctors at the clinic do their part. I'm aware that people don't always agree with Nancy, and we all know she pulls no punches; believe me, she doesn't spare me either. But I can assure you all, the decisions she makes are not for personal reasons but for the good of the clinic.

"It occurs to me that I am now in a strange situation. Instead of being ruled by one lady, I have two now to keep me in check."

He looked at Arshana and everyone laughed.

"I remember when Dr. Taylor said to me, 'David, I have given this matter serious thought. I'm choosing you to continue with my work. You can do it. But you can only do it with the right woman beside you.' I knew exactly what he meant. He had the love and support of his beloved Becky. I'm hoping that with my wife beside me I might do just a little bit of what Dr. Taylor did in his lifetime. There are few people who have given themselves to a humanitarian cause, but Dr. and Mrs. Taylor did.

"I learned a great deal from them and I'm glad that I had the opportunity to know them and be a part of their lives.

"Before I take my seat, I would like to acknowledge the people sitting at my table. The couple sitting at Mrs. Taylor's right are Paula and Robert Romano. After returning from India, Arshana spoke to them about the need for a children's home in the area of Dr. Taylor's clinic. They asked no questions and financed the building of Bobby Romano's Home. And sitting next to Arshana are Doctors Ken and Kathleen Campbell. They are assembling a team of doctors to go to India and do some reconstructive surgery for patients without limbs. Beside the Campbells is Dr. Michelle Mason, a dentist from Ohio. Many of the doctors here have probably read books written by her father, Dr. Errol Mason. Michelle has spent thousands of dollars of her own money to establish a dental clinic in the leper hospital. She goes to India two or three times a year to treat patients… I can see the young ladies waiting to serve us dinner, but I must get let this lady say a few words," he then passed the mic over to Dr. Fine.

"Good evening, ladies and gentlemen," Dr. Fine said as she took the mic. "This is General Fine speaking. I know that is just one of my many names in the office, but I won't mention the others. I can be difficult when things go wrong, but I am proud to say that we have one of the best medical clinics in Mississauga, with doctors who I consider to be the best in the business. I'm excited to tell you about the new doctors we hope to add to our team, but I'm not here tonight to discuss office business. I just want to let members of our staff know that as an extra Christmas bonus, we have come up with a fantastic employment package. I can't wait to discuss it further in the new year. Thank you all," she then returned the mic to David.

When he took the mic, David said, "Just give me five minutes more, please. I know we are all hungry but I must acknowledge two very special ladies sitting at my table: my mother and Becky Taylor, two people who have been great influences in my life. And now I will ask Becky to say a few words."

David helped Becky stand up and he held the mic for her. "Ladies and gentlemen, 30 years ago we had our first Christmas party. There were only six of us then. And tonight, as I look around, I'm amazed at the amount of people here. I can feel Don's presence here with us. It is a sad moment for me, but I thank God that he has left me in the capable hands of Dr. Weissman.

"When Don told me that he had met with his lawyers and handed everything over to David, I couldn't have been happier. Don said that David had learned everything from him, and that he was sure David would do an amazing job. The only thing Don told me he was worried about was David's eye for the ladies. And I said, 'Well he learned that from you, you just said you taught him everything.'

But Don said, 'He'll be so busy running the clinic, I'm not sure he'll be able to maintain his lifestyle. He manages to flirt with so many ladies, I really don't know how he'll keep up with himself."

"Becky, Becky," David interrupted, "Remember your heart, and you shouldn't be on your feet for too long."

"There is absolutely nothing wrong with me. I had my check-up with Dr. Fine last month and she said that I'm fit as a fiddle."

"Mrs. Taylor is in perfect health," Dr. Fine called out. "She is free to talk as long as she likes."

"You guys are enjoying this aren't you," David said. But he was pleased that everyone had relaxed and were having fun, even though right then it was at his expense.

"I panicked when Ruth told me that David had found someone and wanted to get married," Mrs. Taylor continued. "But Ruth told me not to worry. She said I would like Arshana, and she was so right. The first day I met Arshana, I fell in love with her. She's beautiful from the inside out. My life changed as soon as I met her. I now live like a queen. She's made it possible for people to come to my condo and do my cleaning, my cooking or whatever I need to have done. I don't even have to go to the hairdresser, she comes to me.

"David, you couldn't have chosen a better partner and I will continue to pray that your life together will be happy and fruitful."

As soon as she sat down, the waitresses who were standing by began to serve dinner.

Dr. Fine had selected a very nice menu and those who were not pleased with the selection were free to choose something else.

Soft music played during the meal and after dinner, the band prepared to switch to dance music. David asked the band to play I Love You So by Perry Como, and he and Arshana opened the floor. Soon afterwards, several others joined them on the dance floor.

Just before midnight, a dessert table with lots of fresh juice and pastries was laid out. Almost everyone tried the delicious treats and all the guests went home commenting on what a beautiful evening it was.

27

The best part of my day is sitting in my solarium with my first coffee of the day, watching the sun in all its splendor, with all its golden hues. Never in a million years did think I would enjoy living in a condo. But with each passing day, I began to enjoy my condo more and more. Having lived in my home for more than 40 years, I thought nothing in the world would make me move, but with my arthritis getting worse, I found it difficult to climb the stairs. So I switched homes with David and Arshana; they took the house and I took their condo.

I looked at my watch. It was not ticking fast enough for me. Arshana had invited Paula, Robert and I for lunch and I still had plenty of time to get dressed and drive over.

I decided to dress anyway. I got there early and it gave me the opportunity to putter around in the garden.

René was in the garden and he was happy to see me.

"Ma'am," he said, "you have come just in time to see all my flowering shrubs."

"René, I have to admit, I've never seen your garden look so beautiful. Everything is in bloom."

"Ma'am, if you really want to see something beautiful, follow me."

He led me to the rosebush that he and Arshana had planted a couple of years ago. It was laden with roses. Half the branches lay flat on the ground from all the weight, and unopened buds clung to them.

My jasmine tree was also in full bloom; perfuming the area all around the garden.

I picked a handful of flowers and stuck them in my pocket. "Don't look now," I said, "René, your favorite girlfriend is peeping through the fence."

"The witch! I forgot she's moving. I believe that Dr. Chopra has accepted a professor's position in one of the universities in Delhi. I'm sorry to see Dr. Chopra go, but Mrs. Chopra, she can't leave fast enough, as far as I'm concerned."

"Careful, René, you might find someone worse than Mrs. Chopra moving into that house."

"I doubt it, madam, there isn't anyone else like Mrs. Chopra on God's earth."

Just then, Paula and Robert arrived at the gate and René went to let them in. I walked around the house and went upstairs through the back door. I went straight to the living room and was just in time to see David and Arshana welcoming their guests.

A tiny tot with beautiful brown eyes, jet black hair and two of the deepest dimples that I had ever seen fought his way out of Roberts's arms.

He ran through the living room then stopped for a while and looked around. His eyes fell upon the piano that sat in one corner of the room. Solomon had bought the piano several years ago from an antique dealer who claimed that one of the children of the last czar had played it. Whether that was true or not, we never knew, but over the years, that little piano took a lot of pounding from David and his friends. It was painted a gold that hadn't lost its luster after all these years.

Bobby stood for a while checking it over and then he touched the keys with one of his fingers. When it made a noise, he jumped. And then he touched the keys once again. He screamed with delight and looked towards Paula for approval. Paula walked over to him, picked him up and kissed him and said, "I thought my son was going to be a doctor or a real estate broker, it seems he might be a musician instead."

When Bobby saw that he had the approval of both parents, he decided to explore other parts of the house. He went upstairs, checked out all the bedrooms and finally ended up in the kitchen.

René and Betty were there. Betty gave him a cookie and he brought it to Paula and handed it to her.

"See how smart my son is? He never eats a thing unless he gets my approval first."

"Don't you want the cookie?" Paula asked him.

He shook his head and walked over to the bag that held his bottle and tried to get it out.

"He's tired," Paula said. "He usually takes a nap at this time."

Paula took the bottle from her bag and gave it to him, then he walked over to Arshana and smiled at her.

"Would you like me to give you a bottle?" a very pregnant Arshana asked. She took the bottle and Bobby onto her lap. Before Bobby could finish the bottle, he fell asleep.

David carried him to one of the rooms upstairs and when he returned, he said, "I believe we're going to have lunch soon, how about a drink?"

A few minutes later, as we sipped our drinks, Arshana said to Paula and Robert that she had asked them over for a specific reason. Tears filled her eyes when she began to speak. "Thank you both for coming and thank you for being my friends. When I gave Bobby to you, I asked you never to ask me who Bobby's father was and you honoured my request. But you are intelligent people and no doubt you knew all along that David was Bobby's father."

"We figured it out from the first day we saw you and David together," Paula said. She began to cry too.

"You can't imagine how scared Robert and I were, so we pretended not to know anything. We knew that David would have had no problem taking Bobby away from us. Every day was a nightmare."

"David could've taken Bobby back without a problem," Arshana said, "but he knew that if he did, he was going to lose me. So he made his choice, and I hope he never regrets his decision."

Arshana broke down and sobbed quietly.

David couldn't bear to see the woman he loved in tears so he walked over to her, put his arms around her and comforted her.

"Arshana," David said, "don't blame yourself for doing what you had to do. I'm to blame as much as you are. I should have tried harder and done more to convince you of my love for you. I should've stood up for you no matter what."

"Both David and I love you very much Arshana," I said.

"Let's not look back," said David. "We have a beautiful future to enjoy together. We are so blessed to have come together the first time and again, in spite of everything."

"By the way," Arshana said to Paula and Robert, "this is the first time that my mother-in-law has seen Bobby. I hope she will be able to see more of him as he grows up."

Robert and Paula were not opposed to the idea. With everything sorted out, Robert said, "I'm starving. Knowing that I was coming here for lunch, I didn't have breakfast."

Betty prepared an excellent lunch which we enjoyed with a couple of bottles of wine. After lunch, I decided to leave the two couples alone.

I felt a surge of happiness, maybe because I had just met my first grandson and was eagerly awaiting the arrival of my second. I couldn't wait to see David Junior come into the world.

It didn't get any better than this. My cup runneth over.

—

CPSIA information can be obtained
at www.ICGtesting.com
Printed in the USA
LVOW10s1950021117

554723LV00001B/3/P

9 781926 926889